IN THE

SECRET

HEART

From Chris to mom

Read by Eliz. ~~HHl~~ ~~HH~~ I

HHI 12/22
23/21

IN THE
SECRET
HEART

KATHY J. JACOBSON

Kathy J. Jacobson

atmosphere press

Dedicated with love to
Jace, Kendall, and Kennedy

PART I

Millie Paulson wearily patted her face dry with the soft, thick, monogrammed hand towel. Another successful after-Christmas party was "in the books." As the director of St. John's Church choir, hosting this event was Millie's way of saying thank-you to those who faithfully shared their time and talents participating in the Christmas cantata each year.

Millie gazed into the mirror. Her face looked tired and drawn. It hadn't helped that she had gotten everything ready, and cleaned up, all by herself. Her husband, Charles, had called early in the morning with the disappointing news that his flight from Omaha was canceled due to the snowstorm that was just now beginning outside her house in rural Wisconsin. It had socked Nebraska during the wee hours of the morning, leaving her husband stranded. He would be on the first available flight home the next day.

But the party preparations and cleanup weren't the only reasons Millie felt fatigued. She sighed deeply, as the delay meant it would be yet another day until she had the chance to tell Charles her news. She lowered her eyes and her hand slid down the front of the soft, bright red dress she had purchased for the party, stopping just below her stomach, and a smile spread across her face.

She jumped slightly as she heard a little creak. Even though she had lived in this house for years, out in the middle of nowhere, it still made her nervous when she was alone at night. Being alone had become a more regular occurrence lately, as Charles kept advancing in the business world. His trips had gone from "once in a blue moon" to regular occasions over the past six months.

The bones of the century-old abode groaned. On windy nights like this one, the rafters rattled and the cold air whistled through the numerous cracks and crevices, which would cost a fortune to repair.

If not for the weather, the party-goers would have still been around. Normally, they celebrated much later into the night. For many of them, it was one of the few social highlights of the year. But tonight, everyone had wanted to get home before the big storm hit, some planning to stop for a gallon of milk or loaf of bread at the gas and convenience store on the edge of Farmerton before it closed at midnight.

Millie heard another squeak, but dismissed it this time. She lifted her eyes to the mirror again, toothbrush in hand, then caught the sight of another image within. She gasped. It was the last breath she would ever take.

Half an hour earlier

Millicent "Millie" Paulson took one last look around the kitchen and called it a night. The few remaining canapés, decorated sugar cookies, petits fours, and candies were wrapped and put away. Chafing dishes were filled with hot, soapy water and lined the new quartz countertops, soaking away the crusty remnants of her main course offerings. Once again, her recipes had been a huge hit with the members of the choir. It was true that they were an easy crowd to please, not like the discerning palates she had regularly entertained in the Chicago area before she and Charles moved to his family's homestead in Wisconsin.

Each room of the rambling, hundred-year-old stone farmhouse had been checked. Millie picked up stray glasses and pieces of silverware, including a fork which she found strangely sticking out of the dirt of a potted poinsettia plant. She was certain it belonged to Simon, knowing he had had too much eggnog again this year. Thankfully, he had carpooled with some others and wasn't driving home on his own.

Candles had been extinguished and Christmas lights unplugged. Every room had its own uniquely decorated tree and theme. Numerous lighted china cabinets showcased impressive collections of fine Christmas china and other collectibles. Artwork with winter scenes adorned the walls. No space was spared from Millie's Christmas spirit and artistic eye. Christmastime was Millie's favorite season, and she dedicated many hours to making it festive and memorable. Her creativity and energy knew no bounds when it came to two things in life—music and "the holidays." This year, she was feeling even more celebratory, and it showed.

Her guests had wandered from room to room, admiring her handiwork as they sipped hot cider or nog while catching up on the latest gossip and recounting their recent family celebrations. The family tales always made Millie feel a bit melancholy. She had been an only child. Her parents had died in an accident when she was in college, and it changed the course of her life. She had once envisioned becoming a professional singer and had planned to go to graduate school for a master's degree in vocal performance after college. But when they died, she felt lost and uncertain about her future.

She and Charles had only been dating a few months before her parents' deaths, but she had clung to him for dear life after her loss. They had met in the music building at the beginning of the semester. He had been dating one of the young women in the alto section of the women's choir. They bumped into one another—literally—one afternoon as she left the rehearsal room and he was arriving at the door to meet his girlfriend.

Millie had been immediately attracted to Charles, and the feeling was mutual. There was something unique about him—his slender build, sandy hair, light blue eyes, and cleft chin. He wore button-down collared shirts and always had a serious look on his face, which made him look intellectual and intriguing.

Charles thought Millie was the most beautiful girl he'd ever seen, and when he heard her sing a solo from the choir room doorway one day, he was entranced. So after several weeks of trying to pretend they didn't notice one another, Charles broke up with his girlfriend and asked Millie out. They were rarely apart after that.

They were, however, an odd couple. Millie sometimes couldn't understand why they were together—not back in college, and not even after years of marriage. There was the strong physical attraction for certain, but otherwise, Charles was everything she was not, and vice-versa. She was, as Charles referred to her, a "fine arts person," which by his definition meant she was romantic, sensitive, overly emotional, and somewhat disorganized.

Charles, on the other hand, was refined and business-like in every aspect of his being. He was goal-oriented, well-organized, impeccably dressed, dependable, and focused, which was why he did so well in school, and later in the business world. While Millie admired these qualities, she often wished Charles was more spontaneous—and more attentive to her.

Despite their differences—and if she had admitted it back then—and her doubts about him, when Charles proposed the Christmas after her parents' death, Millie answered with a quick and resounding "yes." She felt fortunate. She felt grateful. She felt safe.

The only thing she didn't really feel was love, but Millie convinced herself it would come in time. She had once been in a high school musical production of *Fiddler on the Roof*. She was sure that if Golde could learn to love Tevye, she could learn to love Charles. That was over a decade ago, with no real success in that area.

Millie had hoped things would begin to change when they started a family—but no success in that category, either. Test after test. Doctor after doctor. No definitive answers, although one doctor had a few ideas, which

Charles refused to accept. Millie had wanted to adopt, but Charles didn't think he could "love someone else's child," as he put it. So there they were, in the huge farmhouse Charles had hoped to fill with children—just the two of them.

Part of the reason Charles had wanted to move to the farm after his parents bought a duplex in the nearby town where his sister's family resided was that he had read that stress in women could cause infertility. He thought if Millie—Millicent, as he always called her—got out of the city and could relax more, she might be able to get pregnant. But after years of no results, his hopes for children slowly died.

Over the past couple of years, Charles had thrown himself into his work, which meant he was away more often. And whenever he was home, every conversation seemed to end in tension of some sort—so much for the less stressful environment. After a while, Millie began to look forward to his trips away, as arguing was becoming a too-frequent scenario.

The tension had been even worse at Christmas, when they gathered with Charles' sister and her husband at their house filled with their four children, and Charles' parents doting on their grandchildren. So now, Millie couldn't wait to make her announcement as soon as Charles walked in the door, whenever he finally returned home.

She took one last look around at the quiet house before she headed up the stairs. She went through a mental checklist and was certain she had done everything that needed to be done. She had, except for one thing—she forgot to lock the front door.

Charles

December 29th

Charles Paulson's slender hand trembled wildly as he held his cell phone and called 9-1-1. At his feet lay the cold and lifeless body of his wife, Millicent.

"My wife—she's dead!" he screamed into the phone. The dispatcher calmly asked him to state his name, verify the address, and describe what was happening, telling him to stay on the line until help arrived.

He gave her his name and address, reciting the "fire number" for the rural property four miles outside of Farmerton. With a quivering voice, he tried to describe the scene. The purplish-blue face. No sign of blood. The cold, still body of his wife.

After a few minutes, Charles could hear the wail of a siren in the distance as hot tears came to his eyes. Soon he heard knocking on the door, and the dispatcher gave him permission to hang up.

"What seems to be the problem, Charlie?" asked Sergeant Joe Zimmerman from the County Sheriff's Department, who was stamping snow off of his boots on the rug near the front door. Joe's jacket hung open, revealing a uniform ready to pop its buttons as his bulging belly hung over his wide, black leather belt.

Charles hated being called "Charlie," and Joe Zimmerman knew it. Joe had been a year ahead of Charles in school and the two were as different as night and day. Joe had been a big shot athlete, excelling in football and wrestling. Charles, on the other hand, ran cross-country and participated in the Business Club, school government, music, and plays—less popular activities in this rural community and often considered peculiar, especially by someone like Joe.

"My wife...in the bathroom..." he said, starting to lead the way.

Joe lumbered up the stairs behind Charles, huffing and puffing well before he reached the top of the steep, creaky old oak staircase. He stopped at the landing to catch his breath, then followed the frantic Charles down the hall to the bathroom.

The officer took one look at the discolored body on the floor and nearly lost the lunch he had finally managed a chance to eat. His morning and early afternoon had been spent helping people retrieve their cars out of snowy ditches. He turned his eyes from her face, then forced himself to take a pulse, although he was certain that no one that color could have possibly been alive. No pulse. He pulled out his radio and called dispatch.

"Sergeant Zimmerman here. We've got a corpse. Send out the coroner," he said to the dispatcher, whom Charles had spoken to only minutes before.

"Let's go talk where we have more space and can sit down," Joe said, not wanting to spend more time in the cramped room with a dead body than he had to, feeling a tad faint.

They walked down the hall to the master bedroom. It was a large room with a high ceiling and a huge, arched window that sported an impressive view of the snow-covered backyard. The room was well-appointed, with two high-backed easy chairs in front of a stone fireplace off to the side of the king-sized bed. Two antique dressers and a large bureau lined the walls, as did several oil paintings and two antique photographs.

Joe plopped down into one of the velvety chairs, pulling a small notebook and pen out of his shirt pocket. He still had his jacket on, but decided to leave it. He was hoping to get out of there as soon as possible. This death stuff always made him feel queasy. At least it wasn't a kid this time. His last fatality, the past summer, had been a six-year-old lying crushed beneath an ATV. It still kept him up at night. It was things like that which made him wonder if he had made the right decision in the career department.

"Tell me what happened," Joe said, clicking his pen.

"My flight from Omaha was canceled yesterday. I was going to fly home today, but they had announced the airlines were backed up and it might be tonight, or maybe even tomorrow, before they could fly me out. So when the snow finally stopped around three A.M. and the plows were all out, I decided to rent a car and drive. Maybe it wasn't the brightest idea, but it was better than spending any more time at the airport. So I white-knuckled it back to the Madison airport where my car was parked.

"I got home half an hour ago. Usually Millicent greets me at the door when she hears the garage door go up—she had amazing hearing, considering we have a detached garage. I called for her, but she didn't answer. I thought she might be doing the laundry, but the laundry room was empty. Then I thought she might be taking a nap. She had the big choir after-Christmas party last night, and I wasn't here to help out. She was probably very tired after cooking, hosting, and cleaning up all by herself."

"So, there was a big party out here last night?" Joe

asked.

"Yes, it's an annual event. It is—was—her way of saying thank-you to the choir members from St. John's," he said, his eyes filling with fresh tears.

"How many people would that be?" Joe asked.

"There are thirteen of us—a baker's dozen, Millicent would always say—counting Millicent and the pastor and his wife. It's not a large church choir, but it is for St. John's. It has grown—and greatly improved—since Millicent took over," he said proudly.

They heard a knock on the door downstairs, and Charles ran down the stairs to let the coroner in.

Morris Donner was a grim man, slight of build with greasy dark hair which he wore slicked back. As usual, he was dressed in black from head to toe, with shoes that always looked shiny new. He gave Joe—and pretty much everyone he met—"the creeps." Morris asked Charles the same questions that Joe had asked as he examined the body, and also asked if Millicent had any history of health problems.

After his examination, he estimated the time of death to be at least twelve to sixteen hours earlier, and surmised the cause was strangulation. He told them he would know more after an autopsy. In the meantime, he informed Joe, who was listening from the entrance to the bathroom, that he could now take photos of the scene, after which Joe could help him remove Mrs. Paulson's body.

Joe let out a heavy sigh as he realized he was going to miss his bowling league once again that evening. Instead, he knew he would be interviewing a bunch of "Bible-thumpers" from St. John's. And, worst of all, he had to lug a body down those infernal stairs. *Damn.*

"You mean someone did this—on purpose?" Charles asked in disbelief. "It can't be. Everyone loved Millicent," he said.

"Well, it looks like there's at least one person who didn't," Joe said, "unless there was another motive. Is there anything missing in the house—jewelry, electronics?"

"I haven't had time to look," Charles said, grabbing the bathroom counter. "This is unbelievable." He took deep breaths and steadied himself.

"You go and check the house to see if anything is missing. I'll see if there is any sign of forced entrance anywhere," the officer directed.

"I forgot to mention it—the door was unlocked when I arrived. I just thought Millicent had left it that way for me. She usually makes sure the doors are locked at night, even out here in the country. Years of living in the city created that habit," Charles relayed.

Joe spent the next hour inspecting the house, with one "break" to carry out the corpse, which was now encased in a thick, black body bag and bouncing back toward the coroner's office in the back of Donner's old, half-rusted out Suburban which badly needed new shock absorbers.

As Joe and Charles checked the premises, two other deputies and a Farmerton police officer from town arrived, followed by a state trooper and, a bit later, a news reporter from Madison who had heard the call on one of the many scanners he listened to on a regular basis. As the officers put up yellow crime scene tape around the front of the farmhouse, the young reporter interviewed Joe briefly in front of the stately house. He gave only the few verified details he could share at this time, feeling a bit flustered with a cell phone pointed at him, recording his words.

The deputies seemed to have everything under control, so Joe left the house as Charles began to call his parents and sister to tell them what had transpired. Millie had no family to notify.

***

Darkness began to fall as Joe headed toward town to inform the "church folk." He decided it would be best to begin with the pastor, whose two-story brick parsonage was just a few blocks from St. John's. He could get a list of the choir members from him.

Diane Graves, the pastor's wife, answered the door. She was a petite brunette with long, shiny dark hair pulled back into a ponytail. She still looked like a teenager in some ways. Diane had been one of Joe's classmates. Joe always thought she was a pretty girl back in high school. He had thought about asking her out when they entered high school, but hadn't thought he would stand a chance with someone like her, so he never tried. She was one of those smart girls, always winning some type of award for forensics, music, or academics. They never took the same classes, as he signed up for the least academic courses available. Studying was not one of Joe's strong suits.

Joe sometimes wondered what would have happened had he taken a different path—maybe he could have asked Diane out. One thing he could say about her: she had always been friendly toward him, not like some of the other girls in her clique. She was always kind. She always said hello and smiled at him, and when she opened the door on this day, she did the same.

"Hello, Joe," Diane said warmly. "What can I do for you today?"

"Hi, Diane. It's actually your husband I need to talk to. Is he here?"

She turned around to call Michael, who was already walking into the room, carrying a mug of steaming hot coffee.

Diane turned to him. "It's for you."

"Joe. How may I help you?" Michael asked as he took a step closer, blowing on his coffee.

"I'm afraid I've got some bad news, Reverend. It's your choir director, Millicent Paulson."

Pastor Michael looked up from his coffee mug, a look of concern on his face. "She wasn't involved in some sort of accident on these snowy roads, was she?"

"No—no accident. Ah, I don't know how else to say this, so I'll just say it. Her husband found her dead at their home this afternoon. It appears someone killed her."

Pastor Michael's face turned deathly pale and the coffee cup slipped from his hands, cracking on the hardwood floor and splashing its contents on his brown loafers and the bottoms of his khaki pants. He looked unsteady on his feet, and his wife rushed to his side.

"It will be okay, Michael," she said, grabbing his arm and leading him toward a nearby couch. Pastor Michael appeared almost catatonic. Keeping a hand on her husband's shoulder, Diane turned toward Joe. "Millie has worked at the church a long time. She has been a true blessing to our congregation. She practically resurrected the choir at church. We were down to a handful of us when she came to town." She turned her attention back to her reeling husband, holding his hand. He continued to stare vacantly ahead.

"I'm sorry to bother you at a time like this, but I need a list of all the people who were at the choir party last night," Joe said.

"You don't think anyone in the choir had anything to do with this, do you?" Diane asked. Pastor Michael still sat silently.

"Nah, but I want to ask them if they noticed anything unusual on the property or on the roads in the area when they went home. You two didn't see anything out of the ordinary when you left?" Joe knew from Charles, and from his Grandma's funeral, that both Diane and Pastor Michael sang with the choir.

Pastor Michael, whose eyes now looked red and watery, shook his head. Diane agreed, but did mention that they were in a hurry to beat the snowflakes, which had just started to descend briskly as they had driven back toward town.

"I'll be interviewing each member individually. If you give me the names and contact numbers, I can get a statement from each person and get working on it right away." Joe hoped to be done with his interviews by the end of the evening, if possible.

"Certainly—just let me wipe up that coffee, and I'll be right back," Diane said, rushing from the room and returning with several kitchen towels.

Pastor Michael was still speechless. He was used to dealing with grieving people, but he was not used to being the one who was falling apart. *Who would want to hurt someone like Millie? She was the kindest person I knew. She was so talented. She was...*

Pastor Michael was brought back into the present by

his wife, who sat beside him again, this time holding his arm. He took a deep breath and helped her give Joe the names and phone numbers of the choir members, as most of them were contacts in his cell phone. They were the "worker bees" of the congregation. They were involved in everything and were the heart and soul of St. John's. There was a reason for the saying about "preaching to the choir." They were the ones who "got it," who all knew what the pastor was talking about and tried to live faithfully, within human limits. They were the ones who did the work of the parish. Now, they would be handed this terrible news.

Joe made a list in his notepad and dismissed himself. He had a lot of work to do.

December 30th

Joe wearily forced himself out of bed at 6:00 A.M. He sat up, which seemed to be more and more of an effort with each passing day. He *had* to stop eating and drinking so much. He needed to start working out. He used to be so strong and muscular, now he was huffing and puffing up a single flight of stairs. Yesterday had been a stark reminder of how out of shape he had become.

And being at Diane's house last night really made him feel self-conscious and embarrassed. He thought about Pastor Michael—tall and strong, a full head of hair, and in good shape for someone in his early forties. Someone said he had played college soccer. They didn't have soccer in Farmerton when Joe was in school, so Joe never learned to appreciate the sport. His football teammates and he used to refer to soccer players they saw on television as "lawn fairies." But the pastor was strong, handsome, and, as one of the dispatchers at headquarters had annoyingly mentioned more than once, "hot."

Joe thought again about Diane and how lucky Pastor Michael was to be married to her. Diane had met her husband when she attended a small Christian college in Iowa. Michael was a senior and was accepted into a seminary in the Twin Cities upon graduation. Joe, and everyone in town, was very surprised when Diane married Michael at the end of her first year of college. But she told everyone that all she ever really wanted was to be a pastor's wife and a mom. And both her wishes came to be. Diane and Michael's eighteen-year-old daughter, Addie, was currently off at college at the same school where her parents had met.

Diane had loved being a pastor's spouse, especially in the early years, although she sometimes joked it should be a paid position. She did so much at the church and seemed to be expected to be a part of every committee, Bible study, the women's group, and the choir. She usually didn't mind, as she did love the church, but every once in a while she felt like she needed a break. Recently, this feeling had grown stronger.

As for children, Diane hoped for more than one, but when they hadn't gotten pregnant by the time Addie entered the first grade, Diane went back to school and studied accounting. She had worked part-time for a local CPA ever since. Diane enjoyed getting a paycheck, and also having an excuse to get out a few of the never-ending church commitments.

Joe wondered if he had taken better care of himself, or had gone down a different career path, if he might still be a married man. He thought about his ex-wife, Stacy. She had been the pretty blonde lead cheerleader in high school. He had been the darling quarterback with a bright smile and dimples and a head full of dark curls. They were a striking couple back then, and the envy of many. Now Joe stood up and examined his hairline, which was beginning creep back, and then gazed at his sagging, bulging body in the mirror. He spoke to himself, "I wouldn't want to be married to you, either."

He sighed. He had to report to the sheriff's office and turn in his findings from the night before. He hadn't gotten home until almost midnight. He didn't have much to report. Nobody he spoke with the night before saw anything, everyone had an alibi, and they were the biggest bunch of "goody-two-shoes" he'd ever interviewed. Even so, before he left that morning, he looked over the pile of reports one last time, just to make sure he hadn't missed anything important. He started in the order he had interviewed the members of the St. John's church choir.

The Choir

Edward Knight

Edward closed the door after Sgt. Joe Zimmerman left his immaculate "Cape Cod" on Main Street. He clucked his tongue at the dirty water pooling at his feet, the result of snow that had melted off the officer's boots. "Disgusting man," he said to himself. He walked to the kitchen pantry and brought out a roll of heavy-duty paper towels and began wiping up the mess, displaying his displeasure by hissing like a snake.

He thought about the sloven sergeant's questions. Had he seen anyone or anything unusual on his way home from the party last night? What did he do when he got home? Did he know anyone who might want to hurt Millicent Paulson?

He had had no answers for that loathsome excuse for an officer of the law. He only knew what *he* knew, and he wasn't about to share his thoughts with someone like Joe Zimmerman.

He, Edward Knight, had been the choir director when Millicent Paulson came to town. It was true that when she arrived, he had been toying with the idea of retirement. It seemed like no one wanted to commit their time to the choir anymore. People complained to Edward about his music selections. They wanted to sing more modern pieces—even praise songs. *Praise songs! Beethoven and*

Handel must be rolling over in their graves, he thought to himself. Edward had just turned sixty-five and had no time for all that praise songs nonsense. He couldn't believe what passed for good church music these days.

He remembered when Charles Paulson moved back to Farmerton with Millicent. St. John's was Charles' home church, and they became active members right away, including joining the choir. At first, Edward was happy to have a talented and enthusiastic singer in his group like Millicent, and Charles was a reasonably good singer as well.

But then Millicent began causing trouble. She spoke about how eclectic their church choir's music had been in the Chicago area, where she had served as its director. They had sung every genre imaginable in their worship services. At times, they had even had dancers in the worship service— she referred to it as "liturgical dance"— which made it no more palatable to Edward. Millicent's comments had stirred the already simmering pot of disgruntled choir members and suddenly people were thinking about all kinds of new possibilities. The choir members began talking about using guitars—electric guitars even—and drums, for goodness' sake! *Sacrilege,* in Edward's eyes.

After several months of listening to the choir members whine and plead for change, Edward handed in his resignation. No one even tried to stop him. They had a plaque made for him and served cake the next week during fellowship time to thank him for his many years of service, and that was that. Millicent would replace him the very next week.

Edward was very hurt, but became a member of the

choir nonetheless. He didn't want to let them know how upset he was. He also wanted to show them the level of his dedication to the music program at St. John's. And he also planned to be ready to take over the choir when Millicent fell flat on her face.

But, to Edward's disbelief, that never occurred. Instead, the choir gained several new members and indeed, they sang all kinds of music. He managed to be "sick" or have an out-of-town commitment every time they had a praise song Sunday. He just couldn't get himself to sink that low.

Well, now she's gone, he thought to himself. *Maybe it's God's way of punishing her for the trouble she had caused*, he thought callously. He wiped up one last drop of melted snow and carried the dirty, damp towels to the trash can.

"Goodbye, and good riddance," he said to the garbage—and to Millicent.

Gordon Roth

"You've known the Paulsons how long?" the Sergeant had asked.

"Well—Millicent only since she moved here with her husband. And Paulson," referring to Charles by his surname, "his family and mine go way back—generations."

"Did you see anything suspicious when you left the Paulsons last night? And what did you do after the choir party?" Joe had asked him.

"Like everyone else, I hightailed it out of there before the storm really hit, and went straight home. There didn't seem to be anything unusual at the party or around the property when I left, but then again, I was focused on the weather," Gordon answered. "My wife can vouch that I was home sometime around 11:30."

His wife nodded in agreement when Joe turned toward her to ask. Joe took down Gordon's cell phone number in case he needed more information from him in the future, but Joe doubted he would. These people were some of the hardest-working farmers he'd ever known—good people from a good family.

Gordon saw Joe out of the old farmhouse, and looked around at his property covered with the new coat of snow, which was glistening in the illumination of a huge, bright mercury light. He lived on the family farm—the one his great-grandfather had owned and then lost temporarily during the Great Depression. Gordon's grandfather scraped enough money together after World War II to finally buy it back—at an exorbitant price that had taken everything he had. The Roth family had never truly recovered completely from that loss long ago. It seemed like they worked hard all the time, and still barely made ends meet.

It was the Paulson family who had sold the farm to the Roth family—twice, in fact. The original sale was to Gordon's great-grandfather on a land contract. When the Great Depression hit, the Paulsons, who owned a number of farms they rented out or had sold on a land contract, had given breaks to everyone who was struggling to keep up payments, except the Roths.

There were many stories about why this had happened,

but his grandpa told Gordon once in private it was because of a love scorned. Gordon's great-grandmother had married his great-grandfather instead of marrying a Paulson boy who had been pursuing her. She didn't love the Paulson boy—in fact, she didn't even like him—but he thought she should marry him because he was a wealthy farmer—at least compared to the Roth boys. Gordon's great-grandma had chosen love over money, and it ended up costing them the farm.

Gordon thought about the Paulson family and the way they had treated his descendants as he watched the sergeant walk to his cruiser. *We lost so much because of you Paulsons. So, how does it feel?* He felt a bit guilty, but couldn't help but wonder as he pulled the old storm door shut.

Evelyn Russo

Evelyn sat at St. John's pipe organ, hitting the keys furiously. She played Legeti's *The Devil's Staircase* whenever she was distressed. The news about Millicent's death had sent her to the church immediately following Sgt. Joe Zimmerman's visit to her home. She had barely been able to answer his questions, but had done her best to hold it together as she relayed the story of her departure from the Christmas party with several other choir members in a carpool, arriving home just as the snow storm hit hard.

The piece of music ended and she sobbed. *Why did*

25

things have to turn out like this? She pulled a tissue from the box she kept next to the instrument and blew her nose.

Evelyn had loved Millicent from the second she saw her. She was beautiful. She was kind. She was innovative and smart. Most of all, she was musically talented, and that always made people seem attractive to Evelyn, and was definitely the way to her heart.

Evelyn had tried not to fall in love with Millie, but she had. She found herself more and more often volunteering to play through new pieces, constantly looking for musical works that she thought Millicent might like. They would often stay after choir rehearsal and run through the songs, sometimes for hours. Evelyn practiced for their Sunday morning choir performances, and even for her regular church music, more than she had ever done before, because she wanted to be perfect—for Millie. She had come to the Farmerton area to teach music, but was contemplating leaving for a position in a much larger district when Millie had come to town.

However, Evelyn knew she never had a chance with Millicent. For some reason, Millie seemed devoted to her husband—that weasel of a man, Charles Paulson. Evelyn hadn't liked him from the second he and Millicent moved to Farmerton. She had heard he was a great businessman, a bright star, and a favorite son of the town. People were thrilled when they learned he was coming back and was bringing his wife with him. They were not used to people coming back to Farmerton once they had left, especially those who were working and doing well in a city like Chicago.

But even though Charles was successful, and acted like he was the perfect husband, and they lived in the beautiful, huge farmhouse on prime farmland, Millie never seemed very happy to Evelyn. But perhaps that was because Evelyn never wanted Millie to be too happy—not in her marriage, anyway. If Millie became unhappy at home, perhaps Millie would need her—even if only as a good friend. Thus, Evelyn made it her quest to become Millie's best friend, if she couldn't be anything more. And in Farmerton, one really *couldn't* be anything more, not that Millie had been interested in that kind of relationship in the least.

One night, after one of their long music reading sessions, Evelyn had made the mistake of giving Millie a too-long, too-close hug. It had been a very awkward moment between them, and things had never been the same since. Their nights together at the church had become less frequent and shorter in duration. Millie starting keeping her distance, too. In the past, Millie occasionally sat right on the organ bench with Evelyn as Evelyn played and Millie sang with that voice like velvet. Evelyn was in highest heaven whenever that happened.

But that didn't happen anymore. While nothing was ever said, Evelyn knew she had overstepped her boundaries. She should have known better. She had enough practice over the years hiding her true affections, but there was something special about Millie, and because of that, Evelyn had crossed a line she normally would not have crossed. And now, Millicent was gone. *Forever. For good.* So Evelyn continued to play—and cry—long into the night.

Simon Smith

The officer had asked Simon what time he had arrived home after the party, and Simon told him honestly that he should ask the driver of the carpool, as he wasn't really sure. Simon didn't mention that he was often so intoxicated that he rarely knew what time it was, or if he was coming or going. He had been doing better for a while, but the holiday season always seemed to draw him back into a depressive state. It also didn't help that everywhere he went, someone was offering him a hot toddy or some other sort of alcoholic beverage. He just couldn't say no.

So Simon wasn't really certain what time he had gotten home, or if there had been anything suspicious at the party or afterward. Truly, it was all a blur to him. His only recollection was that the food—and especially the drinks—had been outstanding, but that was all.

Now the officer's words started to sink in. Millicent Paulson, the choir director and host of the party, had been murdered. He walked to the refrigerator and pulled out a beer. It was only noon, but when someone hears about a death—a murder, no less—one needs something to take the edge off. At least that's what Simon always told himself when he wanted a drink.

He wasn't exactly certain how he should feel. He thought Millicent was a good choir director, but he couldn't stand her husband, Charles. In fact, Simon had decided Charles was one of the main reasons he began to drink heavily again—at least that was one of his latest excuses.

Simon had been a real estate developer. It was a great profession in suburban areas, but a lot tougher in a small town like Farmerton. He had been so pleased when it had been rumored that Charles' parents would be moving to another town to live closer to their daughter and grandkids. Charles was off in Chicago, and he and his wife had no children, so the elder Paulsons thought it was a good move.

Simon had pounced on them the second he found out they were thinking of moving. Charles' father was just about to sign on the dotted line to sell Simon the farm. It was several hundred acres, but the most inviting part was a thirty-acre parcel right near the road which Simon planned to make into a housing development. He had the town board on his side, which he had found amazing. He knew the chairman hoped he could get the first choice of six five-acre lots. The rest of the land would be sold along with the farmhouse, which would net him a tidy sum, too.

Then all of a sudden, Charles made the announcement that he and his wife were moving home and buying the entire property from his parents. Charles wouldn't even budge on selling the thirty-acre portion to Simon. Charles couldn't believe his parents had even considered selling any part of the farm a second thought, and had thought Simon to be an unethical opportunist.

And so, Simon lost the biggest deal of his life and had sunk back into alcoholic oblivion ever since. He still went to St. John's, and he still sang in the choir. It was his home church and not even Charles Paulson was going to take that away from him. He rehearsed every Wednesday night and sang every Sunday morning, standing as far away from Charles as he possibly could.

Charles had never even said he was sorry about getting in the way of Simon's deal. It probably seemed like a pittance to someone like Charles, but to Simon, it felt like that deal would have been like finding the pot of gold at the end of the rainbow. It was his chance to make a name for himself (he had planned to name the development Smithfield), and also serve as a nest egg. He could have been retired by now, but instead he would have to work until the day he died. And judging by the way he felt that afternoon, that could be any time now.

Simon crushed the beer can in his large hand and took another can out of the fridge. *Millie Paulson— too bad. Charles Paulson—not sad,* Simon thought as he plopped back into a recliner with his beer.

Margaret Miller

Margaret came into the church office the morning after the officer had stopped at her home. She had reported nothing unusual at the party or on the way home. Evelyn, the church organist, and Simon Smith had ridden with her. Both had been their usual strange selves, Margaret thought, but otherwise, all was good.

She felt so bad for Pastor Michael. He had come in briefly to give her the information for the upcoming Sunday service and some preliminary information regarding Millicent's funeral. He seemed disconnected and not his usual self. He was one of the most positive people Margaret had ever known, and certainly was a breath of fresh air compared to the pastor who preceded him.

But this morning the pastor seemed like a zombie. Then again, this was a pretty unusual situation, and Millie had been a member of the church staff. Margaret liked to think that Pastor Michael would be the same way had something like this had happened to her.

Margaret had been the church secretary since she was twenty years old. Now, at age forty-five, she was still the church secretary. She was good at it, and she knew it. Pastor Michael told her more than a few times every week what a lifesaver she was, and how wonderful she was at her job. She never tired of hearing it, and she was sure she would stay in this position for the rest of her working years—or until Pastor Michael took a new call, whichever came first. She hated to even think about the possibility of him leaving.

He had looked so sad that morning, it had made her heart break. Rarely did he seem as upset over a death as he had with this one. But Millicent had been so young. And it was an unexpected death. Margaret knew from many years working in the church that that always made it harder on those left behind, including the pastor. And again, Millie *was* an employee of the church, after all, and a very talented one at that.

Truth be told, Margaret thought, Millicent was also a very attractive woman. Margaret couldn't help but notice the way men in the congregation looked at Millicent Paulson—even when they tried not to. She even noticed, on occasion, Pastor Michael gazing at Millicent. Margaret didn't really blame him, or any of them, but still, it hurt—

especially when Michael—Pastor Michael—looked at Millicent *that way*. It seemed like that happened more and more often in the past six months, but maybe it was just her imagination—and her longing for him to look at *her* that way—just once. But that was never going to happen.

Margaret fingered her coarse, short dark hair that had begun graying in spots a decade ago. She touched her upper lip, which she had to wax regularly. Although five feet and eight inches tall, she was not willowy like Millicent, and although she was not overweight, she regrettably described her build as similar to that of a linebacker.

"How many copies do you think we'll need?" Margaret asked the pastor.

Pastor Michael didn't catch what she asked and asked her to repeat her question, which she did.

"Millie was so loved. I imagine we will run out, no matter how many you make, Margaret. Use your judgment," the pastor said sadly.

Margaret quietly sighed as she fired up the old desktop computer and got ready to begin the bulletin, wondering if the pastor would be as sad if she were to die. One thing she was sure of, Pastor Michael would never look at her the way he had looked at Millicent Paulson, and that brought tears to her eyes. And she had to admit—she secretly felt relieved, deep down—that he would never look at Millie that way again, either.

Donald Tripp

Donald gazed into the mirror and ran the comb through his recently dyed blonde hair one more time, admiring his reflection. He straightened his tie and tugged on the sleeves of his expensive suit coat. He was due in court in an hour, but needed to go to his office one last time. He had planned to stop there the evening before, but had been rudely interrupted by Joe Zimmerman.

He couldn't get over how Joe had changed from high school. He used to be the envy of all the boys in their class—so handsome, strong, and athletic. Now, he was just a stereotypical overweight cop who looked like he had eaten more than one too many doughnuts.

Donald had been on the team with Joe, but spent most of the time on the bench. He was a late bloomer. He grew four inches in college and didn't really fill out until law school. He worked out whenever he wasn't studying and was at his physical peak when he graduated. Between his new physique and a top-notch position at the largest law firm in the area, Donald made up for his slow start by dating as many women as he possibly could. He thought nothing of going out with two or three of them at a time, making sure to go to movies or restaurants with each in a different community. He started to gain a reputation as a "player" after a while, and he rather enjoyed it. And the women didn't seem to mind, either, as they kept saying yes when he asked them out—or when he asked them to stay the night.

Donald now felt quite accomplished in the romance

area, even though he had one failed marriage and a broken engagement under his belt. Thankfully, none of his relationships had resulted in the birth of a child. He was content with his life at this point in time. He was free. He had money. He had his own law firm. He golfed from spring through early fall and had a membership at University Ridge in Madison, and did a southern gold tour every winter. He had the nicest house on fifteen acres of prime hunting land on the outskirts of Farmerton. He had almost everything a man could ever desire. He could seemingly have any woman he wanted—every woman except Millie Paulson.

She was the only female since his failed attempts to ask a girl out in high school who had ever said no to him. *Who did she think she was?* Of course, she started with the old "I'm married," routine, but so had a dozen other women with whom he eventually shared his bed. He couldn't figure her out. And he couldn't figure out what she saw in Charles Paulson. How could anyone choose Charles over him?

He shook his head as he headed out the door. If Millie had agreed to let him stay the night after the party... His cell phone went off, interrupting his thoughts.

"I'll be right there," he said, and put his phone in his pocket.

And now you're dead.

Janie Johnson

Janie Johnson had been a freshman when Charles Paulson was a junior in high school. Every girl in the school seemed to have a crush on Joe Zimmerman that year—everyone except Janie. She was "in love" with Charles.

There was something about him. He was so smart. He was so interesting. He was so handsome—at least to her. He was tall and lanky—a runner's build. He had long, strong fingers and she dreamed of him running them through her light blonde hair. But he never seemed to notice her—but then again, she had only been a freshman.

Janie used to stop to talk with her friends near his locker, just to watch him out of the corner of her eye and to smell his cologne. He was the only boy in school who wore cologne to class, and she found it appealing—sexy.

She still had a crush on him after he graduated, and was devastated when she learned he was engaged during his college years. She had never completely given up hope on him until she saw the photo of him and his beautiful wife-to-be in their engagement announcement in the local paper. After a year of grieving, she told herself to forget him, and married a young man from Illinois whom she met in college.

Her husband was a nice guy. He did everything right by Janie, but she never loved him the way she had loved Charles. She felt guilty about that throughout their marriage, and especially when her spouse ended up dying in a work accident. He had deserved better than she gave him, and she knew it.

After her husband's death, Janie stayed at her job in Illinois, even though she really didn't need the money. Her husband had invested well. He had also taken out a large life insurance policy, which Janie had thought foolish at the time he bought it. He would always say, "What if something happened to me?" She would shake her head and tell him he was being silly.

But when he died, it wasn't so silly anymore. Because the cause of death was accidental, the payout was doubled, and Janie found herself quite wealthy. While she was trying to decide the best plan for her future, her dad, a heavy smoker despite Janie's best efforts to encourage him to give up the habit, had a stroke, and her mom—a petite woman—needed help taking care of him. Janie really had no good reason to stay in Illinois any longer, so she came back home. And to Janie's great and pleasant surprise, so had Charles. Unfortunately, Janie thought, he still appeared to be married to the beautiful girl in the paper.

And now that "girl" was dead, with a funeral at the end of the following week. Janie thought this was rushing it a bit considering the shocking circumstances, but on the other hand, perhaps the sooner this was done and over with, the better. Maybe then people would stop talking about it, calm down, and begin to put their lives back together and move on. People—*like Charles.*

Jared Jenson

Jared had been shaking in his boots—literally—when the officer from the Sheriff's department had interviewed him. He had stood in the doorway in his blue plaid flannel shirt, Wrangler jeans, and his size eleven square-toed cowboy boots. He didn't really want to let Joe Zimmerman in the door, but he knew he had no choice. He stepped aside, certain Joe was there to question him about the offerings at church.

Jared had been helping count the Sunday offerings during the past year. There were two volunteers from the congregation who did this together after the worship service. Jared was instructed by a man named Edner, who was in his late eighties. Edner's counting partner of many years, Harold, had just passed away, and Jared was his new trainee. Jared had no interest in filling this position, but Edner had always been so kind to him, so he found himself unable to say no when he'd been asked to help.

When the officer began asking questions about the night of Mrs. Paulson's party and murder, he had experienced an inward sigh of relief so heavy he was sure Joe could hear it. Jared had never thought of himself as a thief. He had a job working at a factory. He made a good wage. He had health insurance. He had paid sick leave and time off. He made enough to live decently—but not enough to buy the new truck he really wanted. That was still a few years off, but he wanted it so badly—and he wanted it *now*.

Jared had shocked himself the first Sunday he slipped a twenty-dollar bill into his pocket when Edner had gone to get a refill on his cup of coffee. Edner drank coffee like some people chain-smoked. Jared still wasn't sure why he did it—and why he had continued to do it. What he thought at the beginning was a one-time mistake had now become a regular habit.

He never took more than forty dollars at a time, and sometimes very little, especially if it had been a lighter week of giving and he thought someone might start to ask questions. He stashed the money in various places around his apartment. Somehow it didn't feel like he had taken so much if it was spread around, rather than all together in one place. He had been surprised when he had counted it the last time and it was coming up on two thousand dollars.

He had begun taking extra shifts at the factory whenever he could, so that if he bought his new truck, people wouldn't be as surprised by his purchase. They would just think he used all his overtime pay to put a down payment on it. Everything had been going great—until that morning when Millie Paulson came down the hall, just after he had tucked two bills away.

She didn't say anything or even look at him suspiciously. He wasn't sure that she had seen anything, but he hadn't slept well ever since that morning a few weeks ago. And now she was dead. He felt both relieved and ashamed for feeling that way—almost as ashamed as he was for stealing—from a church, no less.

"So, do you have any idea why anyone would want Millicent Paulson dead?" the sergeant had asked him. He had lied and said he didn't. The officer had wanted to know what time he had gotten home, and if anyone could attest to that. He had been happy to report that his building had a security camera, and that he had gone straight home. He hoped the officer never watched it, however, as he had tripped up the stairs. It was a bit of a miracle that he had gotten home safely, as he was certain his blood alcohol level had been well over the legal limit. He just couldn't stop drinking all that free beer and whiskey at the Paulsons. He had been offered a ride home, but he had to work the next morning and needed his own vehicle to drive to the factory, so he had lied and said he was just fine, and had been on his way.

After the officer had gone, Jared thought about the money—and Millie—and promised himself that this was the end of his crazy habit. He would tell Edner on Sunday that he would have to find someone else to help him count the offering. He would come up with some sort of excuse.

Jared wished he didn't have to set foot in that church again, but there was the funeral the next Saturday and the choir was going to sing a piece. He not only sang with the choir, but also accompanied them on electric guitar occasionally. That was how he got involved with the group in the first place.

The former choir director would lead the choir at the funeral. Jared thought that if Edward took over again in the future, his guitar-playing days with the choir would be over. Everyone knew that Edward hated modern music, and especially hated electric guitars in church. And if he couldn't play guitar anymore, his time in the choir would become a thing of the past.

Jared gathered the stolen cash from a number of hiding places, feeling sick to his stomach as he did so. The truck didn't seem so important anymore, at least not at the moment. It would be awful to burn all this cash, but that was what he felt like doing.

Then he had a better thought. He would anonymously give it to a charity. He thought about giving it back to the church, but he was too afraid someone would figure things out. Instead, he decided he would drop it off somewhere the next time he went into Madison. He would search the internet over the weekend to find the perfect charity. He put the cash away in an athletic shoe box and hid it in the back of his closet. He sighed heavily. *How did everything get so out of hand?*

Oscar Bennet

Oscar had been cooperative with Sgt. Joe Zimmerman, even though the officer had annoyingly arrived during Oscar's favorite television program. Oscar didn't have the ability to record the show—he still used an antenna on top of his roof and his DVR was broken—so that made him even more unhappy.

Oscar told Joe that he hadn't seen anything unusual during or after the party. The gathering had been Millicent's typical extravaganza—lots of fancy food, as he put it. Oscar was a simple person. He grew up eating meat and potatoes, and more meat and potatoes. He did enjoy Millicent's spread, however. He lived alone, so he appreciated not having to cook for himself any chance he got. And it was always tasty, even if he wasn't always certain what it was he was eating. And because Oscar didn't do much in the way of decorating for the holidays, he enjoyed the holiday decor at the Paulson home, even if he would never admit it.

Now, a week later, Oscar was vacuuming the nave of the church. Usually, he would do this on Saturday, but this Saturday was Millicent Paulson's funeral. So now he would have twice as much work to do. He was sure the entire town would be there for the service, which meant he would have to clean up after the horde departed. Because he was singing with the choir, he would have to bring along his work clothes and change into them after the service ended.

It was going to be a very long day for Oscar. There would be the burial in the church cemetery after the service, then a luncheon in the fellowship hall, with people talking and milling about for hours. And then there would be all the flowers that usually made a huge mess. There would be bulletins—and, worse yet, the dirty tissues people would leave behind in the pews. No one seemed to have any respect or consideration for others anymore, Oscar thought.

Unless you were the choir director! People had seemed to fall all over themselves for Millicent Paulson. Yes, she was talented. Yes, she was real pretty. Yes, she got more people to join the choir—especially men, who used to be a rarity. But did that mean she should be treated extra special?

Although he sometimes tried to avoid them, he had attended the last annual meeting of the congregation. Oscar had been stunned to learn of Millicent's salary as choir director. Of course, it was a pittance compared to what she had made in a large congregation in a metropolitan area, but compared to his compensation, it seemed enormous. Compared to her, he was practically a volunteer! It was true, he had often turned down raises in the past, but he had felt hurt and unappreciated at the end of that meeting.

He shook his head as he dusted the window sills. He took great pride in his work—he just wished someone would notice from time to time. It was always Millicent this, Millicent that. She got all the praise. He was forgotten. It had been that same way for him his entire life, in his estimation. No one ever truly appreciated Oscar Bennet. Maybe they would from now on.

***

While the weather system that dumped the fast and furious ten inches of snow had departed, arctic air now invaded Farmerton. Joe opened the steam-covered heavy glass door to the local diner and was hit with a blast of warm, spicy-smelling air. It was minus three degrees outside, with a windchill of much less, but Bud's Diner was going strong. Chili was the special of the day, with a side of homemade cornbread—one of Bud's specialties.

A waitress named Melanie came over and sweetly asked Joe if he wanted the one open booth, or to sit at the counter, as all of the tables were taken. Joe decided on the counter. The last time he tried sitting in a booth he could barely get in and out of it. It had been an uncomfortable and embarrassing situation. There was more space between his billowing gut and the counter, so that settled it.

He ordered the special of the day. He knew from eating

at the establishment almost every weekday that it would be great, and as a special, it would be out fast. Joe was famished. The colder it got outside, the more his appetite seemed to increase.

As expected, the food arrived quickly. Melanie put the steaming bowl down in front of him, along with a square plastic holder filled with packages of saltine crackers. Of course, just as he was about to take his first bite, his cell phone rang. Coroner Morris Donnor's name appeared, so he knew he had to take it, and he reluctantly accepted the call.

"The final autopsy results are in. I forwarded a copy to your office. As I predicted, the cause of death was asphyxiation, in this case due to strangulation using some sort of cloth around the neck. There were no fingerprints, but a few red and navy blue fibers were recovered. The time of death would have been within an hour of the victim's guests' departures. All that was expected. However, there's been a new development. It appears that Millicent was two months pregnant. I'm surprised her husband didn't mention it," Morris said.

"Maybe he didn't know yet," Joe said. He paused. He had a soft spot in his heart for kids, and this made him feel sad. "Gee—that's rough." Joe sighed. He was not looking forward to talking to Charles about this, but he knew he had to do so.

The call ended and Joe had lost his appetite. He was sorry there was a baby involved—so technically, there would be two charges of murder. That also meant more paperwork. And he had to speak to Charles Paulson again, one of his least favorite people in the world.

Joe forced himself to eat half of his bowl of chili, took

two bites of cornbread, left money on the counter to cover his bill and a tip, and was out the door. Even one of Bud's famous homemade pies hadn't tempted him this time. He was actually glad of that, as he was determined now that it was officially a new year, he was going to get back into some sort of reasonable shape and lose some weight.

Joe walked as quickly as he could to his freezing cruiser, the snow and ice crunching beneath his feet. The vehicle's door creaked open and the seat crackled as his body settled into the frigid cold driver's seat. He blasted the heater—at least it was a pretty good one—and pulled out his cell to call Charles, who answered right away. Charles said he would be home— he and his mom were putting together some photo boards for the upcoming visitation and funeral at the church. They were almost done, and then his mom had to go into town to get her hair done at *Sissy's Scissors* for the funeral. Even though she lived in another community, she just couldn't get herself to have anyone other than Sissy do her hair.

They planned to meet in two hours, so Joe headed to the office. He filled his supervisor in on the latest developments in the case, about the new charges that needed to be filed, and with a huge sigh, he began the tedious paperwork.

***

Joe saw Charles' mother, Clara Paulson, drive past him, heading to town as he approached the driveway to the farmhouse. At least the driveway had been plowed this time. It had been a mess the week before. He had examined it thoroughly for footprints, but any that existed had been buried under the deep snow, and later swept away by the high winds that followed the storm.

He just couldn't figure out how this kind of thing could have happened in Farmerton. He knew almost all the people he had interviewed, and even though there were a few he didn't care for particularly, or were newer to town, none of them seemed capable of murdering someone. And no one saw anything out of the ordinary that night. He was sure the weather had a lot to do with that. It had been an awful storm and everyone had been focused on getting home safely.

Charles met him at the door and Joe entered and stopped in the foyer, not wanting to go too far into the house. He hoped to be out of there as soon as possible. Under the circumstances, Joe decided not to be rude today, so he actually called Charles by his given name.

"Charles, I just received the full autopsy report. Not surprisingly, it confirmed death by strangulation, most likely with some sort of cloth. There were a few fibers they were able to find on her neck. But there was something else..." Joe said, hesitating.

Charles looked curiously at him. "What was discovered?" he asked, in that usual arrogant tone of his.

"Did you know—that your wife was pregnant?" Joe asked.

Charles turned white as a sheet, and Joe thought he might pass out. Maybe he should have had him sit down before asking him this question. Joe grabbed Charles' arm. He didn't want to have to get this guy off the floor, or worse, have to give him CPR.

Charles pulled his arm away and shook his head. "We've been trying for years," he said, softly and sadly.

Joe felt legitimately sorry for the guy. "I'm real sorry. We'll be filing a second charge of murder as there was a child involved. Has anything new come to your mind as to who may have wanted to hurt your wife?"

"I can't think of a soul. Everyone loved her."

"Okay. Well, if you think of anyone, or notice anything unusual, give me a call. Again, I'm sorry for your loss— losses. Will you be okay?"

"Yes," Charles said quietly.

"I'll be in touch," Joe said, and headed out the door.

Joe felt bad as he walked to his unit. He didn't like Charles, but no one really deserved this kind of news—not even Charles Paulson.

The new charges were filed, and that meant the media was at it full force. His cell was going off constantly, asking for details and confirmation that Millie had been pregnant. And then he began getting calls from people in town. He was sure that once one person heard about it, everyone would know about it.

Joe thought he should stop by the pastor's house again, as he might want to know about this new development—if he didn't know already via the grapevine—before he presided at the funeral at the end of the week. He slid into the driver's seat, thinking that there was one positive in all of this—he would most likely get to see Diane again.

Diane. Joe had thought about her nonstop since stopping at her house. He thought about her shiny dark hair. He thought about her smile. He thought about how she held her husband's arm in support. *Lucky son-of-a-gun!*

Joe called ahead to the parsonage to make certain the pastor was home. He held on to the rail as he went up the steps to the screened-in front porch, stepping carefully around small patches of ice and snow a shovel had missed. He was wiping his boots on the welcome mat when the door opened, and was thrilled to see the face of Diane.

Today she had her hair down, and to Joe, she looked just like the cute girl he remembered from high school. She smiled warmly at him and invited him in. He stumbled into the house, not because of his clumsiness, but because he was incredibly disarmed by this woman.

Joe stood on another doormat just inside the door, regaining his balance and his senses as Pastor Michael came toward him and shook his hand firmly.

"Any news, Sergeant?" the pastor asked expectantly.

"Nothing about who might have done this, but there has been a new development. It appears that Millie was pregnant—about two months along according to the autopsy."

Both Diane and the pastor appeared badly shaken. Diane grabbed onto her husband's arm, and Joe wasn't sure if it was for her support, or his, or perhaps both. When would he learn to stop telling people things like this while they were standing up?

"Oh, my goodness," Diane finally said. "They have wanted a child for a long time."

Pastor Michael just stared vacantly ahead again.

"Yes, that's what Charles mentioned. It's real sad. Anyway, I thought you would want to know this before the funeral on Saturday. I'm surprised nobody called you yet— it's getting around town slicker than..." He cut himself off as he remembered he was in the presence of clergy—and, even more importantly to him, Diane.

"I've got to get back to work. Just wanted to give you

an update. Sorry to bring such bad news, again," Joe said.

"You were only doing your duty, Joe," Diane said kindly. "We appreciate it."

He almost stumbled out the same way as he had gone in. She had called him by his name. She had thanked him for his duty, which made him feel proud of the uniform he wore, even if it was busting at the seams.

On the way home, he called the local fitness center. He signed up for some kind of special—two sessions with a personal trainer, which probably meant some ripped college kid from UW-Platteville—and three months of membership for only ten dollars a month. Even he could afford that. And he thought to himself, *Diane's worth a lot more than that*, even though he knew she was "taken." Even if she wasn't married, he believed he would have a snowball's chance in hell of ever having anything special with someone like Diane. Although, she did call him by name. She did smile at him. She had thanked him. For now, that was about as good as it got in Joe Zimmerman's book.

***

Joe was positioned in the very back of the packed church the day of Millicent Paulson's funeral. The family had requested the media keep its distance from the church out of respect, but that didn't mean someone wouldn't try. Joe had already escorted one reporter out after attempting to take a photo with his cell phone.

Joe looked around. He didn't care much for church, although he had gone often to St. John's with his grandma. She had been one good woman, and he could never say no to her. Once she went into a nursing home, Joe rarely went to services, with the exception of Christmas and Easter, or a family baptism or funeral.

As Joe surveyed the backs of the heads of those squeezed into the packed, polished wood pews, he kept wondering to himself if the killer might be somewhere in this mob. He couldn't really believe it could be so. In the past week, he had decided that it had to be some freak incident—a random act of violence. It could have been someone traveling through the area, a drifter of some sort, who saw the lights and cars at the stately farmhouse from the road and waited for the guests to leave.

Maybe the person had hoped to steal something—yet nothing had been reported missing from the home. And there were no unusual prints on the property, although it was hard to tell as the snow had fallen so quickly. Then the wind had picked up and drifted in the driveway after the snow stopped falling. Perhaps it was a professional criminal from Minneapolis or Chicago trying his luck in an unsuspecting rural area. He also didn't think anyone in Farmerton was criminally astute enough to pull this murder off so completely undetected.

He had gone to the small hotel in town to see if they had had any guests the week of the murder. There had only been two, as mid-week winter was not a busy time for visitors to the area. If it were summer, there would have been more guests, as tourists came to sample beer at nearby craft breweries, taste wine at several vineyards, canoe or boat on a river, ride the state bike trails, or go to the Dells. At this time of year, however, it was an occasional passerby or a stranded motorist. Both of the people who had stayed had been interviewed, had alibis, and had been cleared.

So, now what? Joe came to attention at the sound of the choir's rendition of *How Great Thou Art,* one of his grandma's favorite hymns. He hadn't heard it since her funeral. He scanned the choir, directed by Edward Knight. The tall, gangly man in an ill-fitting black suit was almost as creepy as Morris Donner.

His eyes moved to the organist, who was situated to the side of the choir loft. She was an attractive woman, but there was something different about her—he just couldn't put his finger on what it was. She sure knew how to play that organ, though. Even someone as non-musical as he was could tell she was a cut above the norm.

After they finished the song, Diane and the rest of the choir took their seats in the choir loft. Joe couldn't keep his eyes off Diane. Even though she looked very sad, she couldn't have looked more beautiful to him, even in one of those silly choir robes.

Once everyone was situated, Pastor Michael walked to the head of the closed casket, which was draped in an elaborate arrangement of red roses with a gold-foiled "Wife" on a large satin ribbon attached. Joe could hear what sounded like a million people sniffling and blowing their noses. He saw Oscar, the custodian and one of the members of the choir, grimace at that, and he didn't blame him.

Pastor Michael, with a somber and somewhat vacant look on his face, put his hand on the end of the beautiful oak coffin. Joe remembered him doing the same thing at his grandma's funeral. Then the pastor did a final com-mendation and benediction, and asked the congregation to stand, if able. The organist began playing a recessional as

Pastor Michael led the procession down the aisle, followed by the casket and pall bearers, then family members. The extra-wide double church doors to the outside were opened wide, revealing the gray and black hearse waiting beneath the church's portico.

The hearse would slowly proceed down a plowed lane to the cemetery behind the church. During the announcements at the beginning of the service, the pastor had cautioned people that the path down to the cemetery could be snowy and icy, and that those who were unable to safely navigate their way could wait in the basement fellowship hall. Winter burial services were a pain, Joe thought to himself. Everything was more of a pain in the winter, for that matter.

Joe watched the faces of the congregants as they passed by. First came Charles, flanked by his mother and father and his sister and her family. They all looked appropriately devastated, and for the second time in a week, Joe felt genuinely sorry for a man he detested.

The choir members followed Charles and his family, several wiping tears from their eyes. The rest of the congregation began to empty out of the pews, some putting on coats to go to the cemetery. Those unable—or unwilling—to make the trek down the snowy hill to the gravesite headed to the fellowship hall to wait and for a cup of coffee.

It seemed to Joe that everyone in town was there. That's what people in small towns in the area did. Even if they didn't know the person who died that well, if they knew anyone in the family, or even a friend of the family, they rallied in support and always showed up. It was one of the things Joe appreciated most about living in a small town like Farmerton, even if he sometimes found it dull and boring. Today, Farmerton was at its best, and he was proud to live there. Yet, there was still the question in the back of his mind—could someone in this nice little town have murdered Millicent Paulson?

A couple of the media outlets from the area wanted to interview Joe after the service, so he didn't stick around for the luncheon. After everyone was settled in for the luncheon, he headed toward the anxious group of reporters who had gathered at the end of the street to wait for him, thinking about how disappointed they would be to find he had no more answers for them today than he did two weeks ago. No one did.

***

Joe finished his media interviews and realized he had left his gloves on the top shelf of a coat rack in the back of the church. He hadn't wanted them sticking out of his pockets during the service, so he had set them there, certain he wouldn't forget them, as cold as it was. But he had been so hot by the end of the packed service that he never gave putting on gloves a thought. When he exited the church, the cold air felt good for once—at least for a short time. During the interviews, his hands had started getting cold, and he suddenly remembered the gloves were still inside on the shelf. He had stuffed his red, stiff fingers into his jacket pockets, trying to hurry the press along. As he walked back to the church building with aching fingers, he cursed to himself.

The warm air felt inviting when he stepped inside the church. Joe could hear the buzzing of voices rising up the stairwell from the fellowship hall. The funeral director stood at a table at the back of the church, sorting out flowers and putting cards, leftover memorial folders and service bulletins, cards, and memorial envelopes into a box for the family to take home with them.

He noticed Oscar standing impatiently in a corner, his chin resting on his folded hands atop a broom handle. He had changed into his work clothes and was waiting for everyone to clear out so he could start cleaning the church. Joe noticed him grimacing every time a leaf or petal fell to the floor from the flower arrangements.

Predictably, the sanctuary was littered with stray bulletins and dirty tissues, another cause for Oscar's demeanor. Joe thought the fallen greenery and trash would be the least of Oscar's worries, though. With all the snow that had been tracked in and melted during the service, there were wet, dirty, and salty streaks every-where—on the oak floors under the pews, down the stairs, and on the carpet. He thought they might have to rent a rug cleaner sometime in the near future, and doubted the church would be in its usual pristine form for the following morning's worship service.

Joe decided he should make a "pit stop" before he headed back on the road, and walked down a hallway toward a bathroom, away from the hubbub. He walked past the empty offices of the secretary and the pastor, both of whom were currently at the luncheon. He made his stop, and was going to go out of the side door when he heard a crash of some sort coming from the choir room.

His hand instinctively settled on the top of his Smith and Wesson .357 magnum, but he quickly removed it and went to check out the source of the sound. Joe approached the choir room cautiously and peered in through the small window on the door. He saw a small table turned on its side, and sheet music spewed across the floor. He didn't see anyone at first, but then he heard someone sobbing.

Joe carefully opened the door and his eyes followed the sound. In the corner of the room, sitting on the floor, with her body pulled up into a ball, was a woman. Her dark curls bounced in rhythm with her sobs. Even though he couldn't see her face, he knew that it was Evelyn Russo, the organist. Her distinctive hair stood out in Farmerton, which was filled with many fair-haired descendants of Germans and Scandinavians.

Joe wasn't sure if he should say anything or not, and decided that he would not bother the woman. She didn't appear to be hurt. He hadn't known she had been so close to Millicent, but then again, she was the accompanist for the choir, so they must have known each other pretty well.

Evelyn didn't seem to notice him, so he quietly closed the heavy door to the room, thinking that Edward Knight would have an absolute fit if he saw that music scattered on the floor. That man was a strange one, and Joe often thought Edward seemed like he had a steel rod shoved up his rear end.

Joe walked back the way he had come and noticed that the pastor's door was now slightly ajar. The lights were off and Pastor Michael was sitting at his desk, his head in his hands. Joe didn't want to bother the pastor, so he quietly continued on to the exit.

His stomach growled as he walked down the sidewalk to the street, reminding him he hadn't eaten lunch yet. He hopped into his cruiser and headed for Bud's, wondering what the special of the day would be.

Bud's was the emptiest he'd ever seen it. There was one waitress, one cook, and one customer. Bud had almost closed the place for the day, but he had found two workers who volunteered to work and miss the funeral. The special was chicken noodle soup and a salad, and Joe decided it fit well with his new healthier eating plan. He had actually lost three pounds in the past week, which, while not a lot, was a start.

Joe took a seat at a table, and as he did, people started trickling in, some coming from the funeral lunch just to have a cup of coffee and, more importantly, to gossip about all that had just happened. Joe knew the three men, still in their suits, who had taken seats at the lunch counter. One was in a suit so old and worn that its material shone. Joe recognized him as a Roth—Gordon's uncle, Jon. Joe thought again how that family worked so hard, yet never seemed to get ahead.

Joe finished his soup and salad and walked over to talk to them. If nothing else, it would keep him from ordering any dessert. The men were discussing the service, which gave him a perfect segue into the conversation.

"Wasn't that choir something?" Joe asked nonchalantly.

"Yes, that Millicent really whipped them into shape. It's too bad that pasty corpse, Knight, will probably take his old job back. He's probably happy about that—he never liked Millie very much," said Jerry Jones, the manager of the feed mill and a man with absolutely no personal filter.

"Why do you say that?" Joe asked.

"Didn't like that modern music she picked out," he continued. "Jealous, too," he tacked on.

"Well, she pretty much swooped in here and took over," Jon said. "Typical Paulson maneuver," he said with a slight frown on his face.

"I thought everybody loved her," Joe stated. "The church was packed."

"Most did," the third man, Mason Marks, chimed in. "Not everyone loved her husband, though."

Joe saw Jon Roth nodding at that, and found himself nodding along, too, as he was one of those in the club who didn't care for Charles Paulson. He quickly stopped his nodding, as it didn't seem very professional, and he changed the subject.

"And how about that organist?" Joe mentioned, wondering if the men could shed any light on her earlier behavior.

"She sure can tickle those ivories," Mason said, "but she's an odd one."

"She's a real looker, though," said Jerry.

"Well, she's not your type, Jer—she's not anybody's type—at least not any *guy's* type, if you know what I mean," Jon shared.

"Really? How would you know?" asked Jerry.

"My wife is a hairdresser. She knows everything. You want to find out information—go down to Sissy's and you'll get your answer," Jon said, sounding proud.

"Damn!" exclaimed Jerry.

"You're too old for her, anyway," Mason kidded him. "And how's that wife of yours these days?"

Jerry turned a deep shade of red and changed the subject again. "Never seen so many flowers at a funeral before," he remarked.

"What a waste of money!" Jon added, as he always had to carefully manage his pocketbook.

"I bet ol' Oscar is having a hissy fit. All those flowers—

and the snow and mud everyone tracked in to church, too! Last year he went off the handle at the annual church meeting about how he doesn't get paid enough for what he does, especially compared to people like Millicent. He was real angry. I thought he was going to up and quit. Pastor Michael had to take him into his office until he calmed down," Jerry added.

The men finished off their second cups of coffee and decided they had better get back to work. Joe decided he'd best do the same, although in some ways he felt like he had been working already. Joe had just learned more in ten minutes at the restaurant counter than he had in the entire past two weeks of investigation.

***

Joe went back to his office, took a sheet of paper out of the copy machine, and made some lists. He put Millicent on one side, Charles on the other side, and started to put names in each column of people who might have had a grudge against either one of them, or both.

He looked at it when he was done. True, these people may not have liked these individuals—but was it enough that they would kill over it? He just didn't see how it was possible, but he folded the sheet of paper and put it in his pocket anyway. He would add to it as he discovered more. No one else was coming up with any answers—not even the big shots from Madison who always thought they knew everything, nor the reporters who sometimes came up with things no one else uncovered or thought of. No one had a clue this time, so Joe didn't feel completely incompetent, just weary.

When his shift came to an end, Joe started for home. His route took him past the church one last time. Oscar's car was still there, as was Charles Paulson's white SUV, and another black car he didn't recognize, with someone sitting in the driver's seat.

One of the church's doors opened and Charles walked out. As he approached his vehicle, the driver's door to the unfamiliar car swung open and a woman popped out. She wore a stylish, long black wool coat, a stocking cap, sunglasses, and her long blonde hair blew around her face in the winter wind. She approached Charles and he looked startled. She walked up to him and threw her arms around him, giving him a hug.

Charles pulled her arms down from his neck and stepped back. Joe couldn't see what he said to her, but he didn't look very happy. Charles quickly got into his vehicle and started it, the woman watching him as he backed up and turned his vehicle to exit. The woman smiled, waved at him, and shouted something. Charles did not return her wave, which made her look a bit silly to Joe. She looked familiar, but Joe just couldn't place her.

Joe continued home, wondering what all that had been about. Finally, he entered his small house, changed clothes, and washed his hands. He wanted a beer out of the fridge so badly, but he resisted. Instead, he went to his second bedroom, where a brand new weight bench and weight set were waiting for him.

"Never put off to tomorrow..." he said to himself, quoting his grandma. She never finished the sentence— just said those words, which were enough. She always followed through on whatever she needed to do, and Joe was determined to do the same.

Joe lifted and grunted away for the next twenty minutes, doing some of the exercises he had learned at the gym. He would have done a longer routine, but he didn't want to overdo it and use sore muscles as an excuse to stop working out. He got up from the bench, wiping the dripping sweat off of his face and arms with an old kitchen towel. And just then it dawned on him—the woman in the church parking lot. It was Janie Johnson.

Janie had been behind him in school—he couldn't remember exactly which class, but she was always hanging around the upperclassmen. She was pretty, and she knew it. Her long, blonde hair and bright blue eyes turned a lot of heads, except his. He was "taken" at that point by his future ex-wife, Stacy, already talking about their someday wedding since their junior year. He couldn't believe it, looking back, that he could have been so foolish to commit to someone at such a young age.

But Stacy—Stace, as he called her—was beautiful. She was a cheerleader and leader of the squad, which at their school had been a big deal. She was going to be a dental hygienist, and had a smile that could serve as a walking advertisement for any dentist's office. Stacy was all signed up for the area technical college and started taking classes their senior year, and graduated from her program a year after their high school graduation. Joe had a year of law enforcement training at the tech school when he jumped on an opening at the sheriff's office. They paid for the rest of his program and Joe had the job of his dreams. Joe and Stacy got married. Everything had seemed so perfect—in some ways.

Stacy had their future all mapped out. School—jobs—marriage—kids. It was the way it was supposed to be, she told him, and he had believed it. But Joe felt like every second of his future was planned out for him, and then he started to feel resentful and like he was suffocating. He began staying out late with other deputies when they got off after the three-to-eleven shift. He started to gain weight, eating and drinking his feelings rather than sharing them with Stacy.

Joe wasn't ready for children. He wanted kids in the future, but not when he was twenty years old. Eventually, they drifted apart, and Stacy became less and less attracted to him as he became less and less attractive, both physically and emotionally. They argued, and then they stopped talking altogether.

When a new dentist set up a practice in a nearby town and offered better wages, Stacy left the small dental office in Farmerton, grateful for the opportunity. She found not only a new job, but a new man, the dentist. Dr. Casey was more mature, made a lot more money than Joe ever would, and was ready to settle down. So as Stacy became less attracted to Joe, she became more attracted to her new boss. Just before their third anniversary, she moved out. A few months later, she filed for divorce, and six months after that, she married the dentist. Within a year, she became the mother of the first of their three kids.

Sometimes Joe felt that perhaps he should have just had a child like Stacy wanted, but he knew from his work that unwanted children's lives didn't turn out so great. Yet there were times he wished his life was different than it had turned out to be. He always thought he would have found someone else to settle down with, to have a family with, but it never materialized.

Joe got himself a cold glass of water from the kitchen

tap, then plopped down in his recliner in his living room. "Janie Johnson," he said out loud. She was one of the choir members he had interviewed. He thought back to high school. He remembered Janie had often hung around Charles, but he just wasn't really into her. In fact, Charles didn't really date, rather he was in a group of junior and senior students comprised of musicians, actors, and National Honor Society members, which included Diane. The cohort tended to do things in tandem, like go to movies in Madison or even school dances.

How Charles got so lucky in high school, Joe never understood. Then Charles went away to college and came back years later with a beautiful wife. Again, Joe could never quite figure out how Charles managed that. But now that beautiful woman—Millie—was dead. And there was Janie, hugging Charles in the church parking lot. Joe decided he'd better check it out the next day.

***

Janie Johnson opened the door, flipped back her long blonde hair, and flashed a smile, just like she used to do in high school. *She's still a player*, Joe thought. And she was still beautiful—there was no doubt about that.

He lied and said he was doing follow-up interviews with the last people to see Millicent Paulson alive, and asked if she had thought of anything else since their initial conversation. She said she hadn't. Then he asked her how well she knew Charles Paulson.

Janie's smile faded. "We see each other at church and choir, of course, but rehearsals and services don't include a lot of conversation. Outside of that, we see each other on the street or in the store occasionally, but he always seemed to be in a rush. I tried to talk to him yesterday after the funeral, but he was a bit beside himself," she said, sounding defensive and obviously disappointed.

Joe felt a bit disappointed, too. He thought she would try to hide the conversation—or whatever it was—with Charles, but there she was, talking about it. Joe had suspected the two of them were more than just friends from choir, but now he wasn't getting that vibe, even though he was pretty certain Janie would like it if they were. Joe wondered if that would be enough motive for Janie to hurt Millicent. He scanned her body—all five feet six inches, one hundred and fifteen pounds of it. Would this woman be able to strangle Millicent? He highly doubted it.

Janie noticed Joe looking her up and down, flipped her hair once more, and smiled. "Would you like to come in?" she asked.

Joe hadn't had an offer like that in a long time, but there was something about Janie which he found unattractive, even though she was very pretty. Plus, he was on the job.

"I've got work to do," he said, taking a step back from the door and Janie and turning to go.

"See you later, Joe," Janie said, making it sound more like a question than a statement.

"Later," Joe said, and then regretted the possible implication of using that word.

Janie closed the door. What should she do now? What was it her mother used to say—the way to a man's heart was through their stomach or something like that? She decided she would cook the only really good dish she knew how to cook—a chicken and noodle casserole—and she would take it to Charles. Maybe he would appreciate that more than the hug she had given him. It had probably been too much, too soon. But she had made up her mind. She was going to have Charles Paulson if it was the last thing she did in life.

***

Joe felt discouraged when he arose on a cold Wednesday morning. He seemed to be coming up with dead ends everywhere he turned. His mind turned back to his thought that perhaps this was someone from out of town, and then he remembered something. Charles and Millicent had lived in the Chicago area before moving to the farmhouse. Maybe he should be talking to some of the people who knew her there. He would get right on it. He was so excited by the idea that he didn't even curse at the freezing cold as he jumped into his cruiser, or the snow that was beginning to fall once again.

Joe's excitement fizzled as the day wore on, however. He spoke with the music director at Millicent and Charles' former church in Naperville. The director had nothing but glowing things to say about her. He was very helpful with contact information for others who knew her, as well. Each person, whether it was a friend or someone she worked with at a center for fine arts, all gave equally positive reports. Many were shocked to hear she had died, and were sad to have missed the service for her. Joe was surprised that Charles hadn't informed more people, but perhaps they had been gone from that area for enough years that it slipped his mind to let more people know what was going on. Or maybe he had been in too much of a state of shock, which would be understandable.

Joe's phone died just as he ended his last call on the list. He attached it to a charger and sat back at his desk, taking out the piece of paper with his lists. He added all the names of the people he had contacted that day. At least it made him feel like he was trying, even if he hadn't learned anything new. Millicent was a beloved person. No one could believe anyone would want to hurt her. If he hadn't seen her dead body with his own eyes, he might not have believed it himself.

Joe used the restroom and looked in the mirror as he washed his hands. His hair was getting a bit shaggy, but he noticed for the first time that his face looked thinner. "Well, I'll be damned," he said to himself. His uniform fit better and it didn't look like a button might fly off at any moment anymore. He stood up straight, feeling a bit proud, and ran his hand through his hair. He should go to the barbershop—but then had another thought. He wasn't looking forward to it, but Joe decided he would use his afternoon break to get a haircut—at Sissy's Scissors.

***

Joe almost turned around to leave after he opened the door and stepped into Sissy's. There was some sort of strong chemical smell in the air, and six pairs of eyes were glued on him.

"Can I help you, Joe?" Sissy asked as she wrapped bits of a woman's hair into what looked like tin foil to Joe.

"Any chance I could get a quick haircut?" he asked, almost hoping she would say no.

"Anything for an officer of the law," she said. "Honey," Sissy said to a young stylist next to her, "you take over here and I'll do the cut." She led Joe to the one open chair in the room.

Joe sat down and Sissy put a brightly-colored cape around his shoulders. If he could have run away, he would have. Why he had thought this would be a good idea, he now had no recollection. He practically squirmed in his seat.

"What are we doing for you today?" Sissy asked. Joe had never been asked that in his life. He always just sat down in a barber chair and it was the same cut every time.

"Just a haircut."

Sissy smiled. "Okay, that I can do."

After Sissy got underway, the place went back to its normal chatter.

"I hear the choir at church is starting practice again tonight," one woman said. "Edward is taking over."

"He must be thrilled," another woman said. "He never liked Mrs. Paulson's way of doing things."

"Yes, he was very unhappy with the group after she took over," the first woman replied.

Another woman jumped in, "He is jealous of her—*was* jealous, I mean."

"I thought maybe that organist would take over. She teaches music to the kids at school—she probably wanted the choir at church, too."

"Let's change the subject, shall we?" Sissy suggested. Personally, Joe hoped they would keep talking. That was the only reason he had propelled himself into this embarrassing situation.

"I just can't believe Millicent is gone," the first woman

said.

"Who would want her dead? Everyone loved her," another said.

"But did she love everyone? How about that pompous Donald Tripp? He was always throwing himself at her, even though she was a married woman!"

"Donald throws himself at every woman, married or not—he thinks he's God's gift to us," another woman mentioned.

"Speaking of throwing oneself at the opposite sex, there's that Janie Johnson."

At the sound of her name, Joe could feel the red crawling up his neck to his cheeks as he recalled her recent "throw" at his very own self.

"She'll probably be all over Charles Paulson now that he's a widower."

"I remember back in high school how she liked the boys—especially Charles."

Sissy had been quiet for the most part, but chimed in when the subject turned to Charles.

"I don't know what anyone would find appealing about Charles Paulson, or anyone in the Paulson clan. They are arrogant and uncaring people going back generations. Just ask my husband about how the Paulsons treated the Roths in the past," she said with a sharp tone. Joe's ears perked up at this, and he wondered what had happened between the Paulson and Roth families in the past. He made a mental note to find out.

"Okay, new subject," someone else said. "Are you ready for the Fireman's Snow Ball?"

The conversation now revolved around new dresses and shoes, and making sure they had hair appointments that morning for hair and makeup. The Fireman's event was the biggest fundraiser for the Fire Department and actually had a great turnout, as there was a live dance band hired and catered food. It was definitely the biggest night of the winter in Farmerton.

Sissy whipped the cape off of Joe's shoulders. "There you go," she said.

Joe hadn't really been paying any attention to what Sissy was doing. He had been too intent on listening to the conversation. He did a double-take in the mirror. His hair was about the same length he normally had it cut, but there was something different about it. The shape—he guessed they called it a style. It made his face look thinner and he thought he might even look younger.

He stared more, and Sissy noticed. "Is it okay?"

"Yeah, thanks," he said, still amazed at her work. "What do I owe you?"

"On the house," she said.

"No can do," Joe said. "No offense—it's just department policy."

"Then pay me whatever you normally pay for a cut," she said.

Joe gave her a bit more than he normally paid, and tipped her well.

As uncomfortable as he had felt at times, Joe left the shop feeling like a new man. He liked the haircut, and he had actually learned that not everyone loved the Paulsons. At least it was *something* to work with.

***

Over the next month, Joe investigated more thoroughly all the possible "suspects." He even went to church a few times to watch some of the choir members interact—and in the end, he came up with a big fat zero. Everyone seemed to be moving on and acting in a reasonable fashion. Everyone still had alibis for the night of Millicent's death and none of the motives he had learned about seemed strong enough to elicit the act of killing Millicent.

It was a frustrating time for Joe—except in his personal corner of the world. Joe had become more and more motivated by his weight loss ever since that day he had gone to Sissy's. Other people were beginning to notice his progress—like the dispatcher at the office and even his superior officer. And, best of all, Diane, who complimented him one day after church.

He was on the last hole on his belt and had given two of his uniforms to a woman at church who did alterations. He thought he might have to break down and actually buy some new ones, and other clothes, sometime soon. Joe hated to part with that kind of money, but it still made him feel good inside. And to top it off, he felt better in general than he had in years. His energy level was up, and the more weight he lost and the more he worked out and turned flab into muscle, the more he felt like exercising and being more active in general.

Still, he found this unsolved case to be unsettling. Joe went back to his idea once more that it was someone from outside the area. He ran a search on strangulation deaths that had occurred in the past six months, then during the past year. He looked at data from the state, then the entire Midwest region, and eventually the entire nation. He hoped to discover some cases with similarities, but there were no close matches or patterns he could detect. This was a real mystery to him, but he just couldn't move on, even though his superiors were starting to indicate he should spend less time on the case.

Joe put his feet up on his desk, his tactical side-zip boots clunking on the metal desktop. He put his head back and had just closed his eyes when his cell phone rang, causing him to nearly fall out of his chair in a start. When he finally recovered, he saw Diane's name flash on the front of his cell. He hunched over the desk and accepted the call.

He decided he wanted to sound professional when he answered, so he used his formal voice. "Sergeant Joe Zimmerman. How may I help you?" he asked, pretending to not know who was on the other end of the line.

At first he thought she must have dialed his number by mistake, as there didn't appear to be anyone on the line. But then he heard a whimpering sound.

"Hello—is anyone there?" Joe asked.

Then a faint voice said, "Help."

"Diane—is that you?" Joe asked, fear rising and adrenaline beginning to pump in his body.

"Help," the voice said again.

"Stay on the line," he said to the voice. "Are you at home?" he asked. There was a faint "Yes."

"I'll be right there," he said, putting on his jacket and grabbing his phone. Luckily, Diane's home was only minutes away.

He debated whether or not to use lights and sirens. Then again, Diane—or whoever was on the other end of the line—hadn't called 9-1-1, but had called his personal phone number.

Joe began to wonder if he shouldn't have some sort of backup. What if this was some type of setup or something?

The events of the past two months had him on edge and thinking about things he had never even contemplated before in his usually quiet, sleepy little hometown.

But as Joe climbed into the cruiser, he decided he would just take his chances. No siren. No lights. No backup. Besides, he didn't want to get to Diane's and find out there was no emergency and look like a fool. Not in front of anybody—but especially not in front of Diane.

It was a sunny and mild day. There was a bit of a thaw going on, as snow melted off rooftops and small rivulets of water cut tiny streams in the packed snow on the sides of the street. Even though it was only thirty-three degrees, comparatively it felt balmy. Joe hadn't even zipped his jacket or put on his gloves or hat. He parked his cruiser in the slushy snow at the curb and headed to Diane's door. He decided to call his dispatcher and tell her he was going to the pastor's home to follow up with someone on the Paulson case. He thought that if he wasn't heard from after a few hours, at least someone would know where to begin looking.

He knocked on the door, but there was no answer. Now he started to worry again. He knocked harder—still no answer. He tried the door and it was unlocked.

"Hello, Sheriff's Department," he called out.

He heard whimpering again, then the faint voice. "In here," he heard.

His heart began beating against his chest, and he drew his weapon, holding it down at his side. He was a pretty quick draw, so felt confident that if he needed to use it, he could still do so quickly enough. He scanned the foyer and it was clear. He moved past it, then saw Diane. She was sitting on the floor at the bottom of the staircase, holding a piece of paper in her hands and crying softly.

Joe took a few steps forward and stopped dead in his tracks. "Holy sh..."

First he spied the brown leather loafers. His eyes moved upward to the khaki pants and the light blue dress shirt, then to the face. It was Pastor Michael, his limp body hanging from the railing of the staircase, a red and blue striped tie around his neck. A small step stool laid on its side near his feet, which were barely off the ground, but just enough to achieve the goal.

Joe walked slowly toward Diane, stopping at her feet. She finally looked up, her swollen red eyes meeting his own. She didn't speak, but shakily handed him the paper she had been holding.

Joe silently read the typed words on the page.

```
Dearest loved ones —
   I cannot live with myself or my secret
any longer. I am responsible for Millicent
Paulson's death. I have sinned and fallen
short of the glory of God — and also of
your love and trust. I pray for God's for-
giveness, and that one day you will be able
to forgive me for my actions as well. I
love you all, especially my beloved Diane
and sweet Addie. You deserved better.
```

Joe could barely believe his eyes. Of all the people in Farmerton, Pastor Michael would have been the *last* person he would have ever expected to have killed someone, or himself. But Joe also knew from years on the force that sometimes things—and people—were not as they seemed.

He folded the paper and put it in his pocket. He called

the dispatcher and went to Pastor Michael's body to check for a pulse, but for the second time he was pretty sure there was no way a person could be alive and look like that.

As suspected, there was no pulse. He called the dispatcher and gave her directions, then backed away from the corpse and turned to Diane, extending his hand to her. "Do you think you could stand up and we could go to another room?" he asked gently.

She nodded affirmatively, and he began to pull her up. She stood and stumbled forward a bit and he caught her. He could smell her hair, and held her tightly until she regained her footing. He was so glad he was in better shape as her body pressed against his. When she seemed stable, he guided her to the kitchen table, pulling out one of the heavy wooden Amish-made chairs for her to sit in.

"What can you tell me, Diane?" Joe asked.

"Today was quilting at church—we make them to give away," she said, dazed. "Michael knew I wouldn't be home until after lunch—we always have a lunch after we're done quilting..." She paused, tears rolling down her cheeks. "When I got home—there he was."

Just then the ambulance and another squad car arrived. Joe rose to meet them, but got Diane a glass of water before he left the room.

The EMTs ran into the home, but slowed down when they saw the pastor's limp body and discolored face. They confirmed there was no pulse and left the body as it was for the coroner. The other officer began to take photos of the scene, and the coroner was on his way. Joe told the officer about the suicide note, and took a photo of it with his phone just in case anything were to happen to it.

Morris Donner arrived. He still made Joe cringe. *Why*

was his hair always so oily?

"We have to stop meeting like this," Morris quipped. Joe didn't find it remotely funny to joke at a time like this, especially as the dead man's widow had just come back into the room.

"I'd say he's been dead a few hours. You say there's a note?"

Joe handed it over momentarily. It was not handwritten, so it would have to be checked against a computer at Pastor Michael's home or office, just to make sure he actually wrote it.

"He did this just right. If he would have gone higher up the railing, the tie probably would have broken under his weight," Morris went on.

Joe looked at Diane, who was white as a ghost. "Diane, let's go back into the kitchen."

"No, I want to hear what he has to say."

"There isn't too much else to say. It seems pretty cut and dried, unfortunately. If you have all the photos you need, we can take the body for autopsy."

Morris motioned to the EMTs to help him. And even though Joe was in better shape on this occasion, he felt relieved he didn't have to remove another corpse. And most of all, he didn't want to leave Diane—not even for a minute—in her current state.

For a second time, Joe guided Diane to the chair at the kitchen table. Diane looked straight ahead without blinking an eye.

She finally spoke. "How could he?"

Joe actually had been asking himself the same thing—in more ways than one.

Diane continued. "I went to bed as soon as we got

home from the choir party. I was very tired and fell right asleep. Michael went to his study to do his bedtime devotion and prayers, like he always does. Not even a late night keeps him from reading the Bible and praying for the members of the congregation."

The wheels of Joe's mind began to turn. The pastor must have gone back to the farmhouse, knowing Millicent's husband wouldn't be home until the next day. But still, why would he want to hurt her?

"It's hard to know what goes through people's minds sometimes, Diane. I see it all the time—people doing things one would never expect."

She nodded, her eyes welling with tears again.

"I hate to bring this up at a time like this, but do you think your husband used your home computer or another one to write the note? I just have to verify it."

"I'm not sure," she said. "You can check in his study. It's just off the living room—the small room with all the bookshelves and a desk."

Joe put his hand gently on her shoulder as he rose. "I'll be right back."

He easily found the study and the computer. There was paper in the printer and he took a piece, then unfolded the paper Diane had given him. They didn't seem the same, but he took the piece to make sure. He'd have to go to the church next, but thought about Diane.

He came back out to the kitchen. "I'll have to check at the church. I don't think it's a match with the paper in the study. Diane—is there someone I can call to come and stay with you?"

"I don't want anyone here. I have to call my daughter— and I need to be alone when I do that. Then I have to tell his family, and my parents. If I need someone afterward, I have a friend I can call to come over later—but I just can't face anyone right now—not under these circumstances."

Joe nodded his head in understanding. "It had to be quite a shock."

"It was."

"I will call you later, if that is okay?" Joe asked.

"That would be nice. Thank you for your kindness, Joe. I'm so glad I called you—and that you answered."

"Me, too," he answered sincerely. He gave her shoulder a little squeeze and headed for the door.

As Joe slid into the driver's seat of the cruiser, he couldn't help but ask out loud, "What the hell is going on in this town?"

***

Margaret Miller had been a basket case when Joe Zimmerman left the church office. She figured out that something terribly wrong had happened almost as soon as he stepped foot in the door. She wouldn't allow him to look at the pastor's computer or cooperate unless he gave her at least some indication of what was going on. By the end of his time there, she knew most of the story. He was pretty sure it was all over Main Street already, as there were many people who listened religiously to the police scanner.

He took some of the paper from the pastor's desk next to his printer. It seemed to be a perfect match. He looked around for a password for the computer, and after he gave up his search, he finally convinced Margaret to give it to him.

There was nothing in the document file or on the desktop, but then he checked the "trash." There was an unnamed document that hadn't been deleted yet—and there it was. The very words he held on the note in his hand, right there on the computer—Pastor Michael's note. He copied it off, and also took a screenshot of it. Then Joe told Margaret that no one should touch the computer, or anything in the pastor's office, until further notice.

Margaret had been sobbing when he left, and Joe felt terrible. And he knew it was only the beginning of many tears that would be shed. The church would be in upheaval now. First, the choir director, now the pastor—two beloved people gone for no good apparent reason. He wondered what the reason was. Why would Pastor Michael want Millicent dead? Had she discovered something about him he didn't want others to know about? Was it a work squabble? He doubted any kind of disagreement about work would be bad enough to kill someone for—then kill oneself—but who knew anymore. Joe felt like he didn't know anything about anyone or anything anymore. This whole winter had been one big crazy mess. He only hoped he could find some clarity at some point—for sanity's sake—and most of all, for Diane's sake.

***

Joe laid in bed that night staring at the ceiling until the early morning hours. Adrenaline coursed through his body. Another dead body. Grieving people. Diane.

Diane. He couldn't get the scent of her hair out of his nostrils. He swore he could still smell her; could still feel her body against his. He could feel her shoulder under his hand. He could hear her voice thanking him.

Joe had called Diane early in the evening to make sure she was okay. Her daughter had just arrived home, so she could only talk for a moment. She thanked him profusely again. She also told him that she and her daughter, her parents and Michael's parents, and his sister and her family were going to have a private graveside ceremony in the church cemetery where Michael's grandparents and other family members were buried, a few hours north of Farmerton. She said she just couldn't bury her husband at St. John's after all that had happened. Then Diane shocked him by inviting him to attend, but said she would understand if he couldn't come on such short notice, and with it being so far away. He told her he'd get back to her on that.

So now he couldn't sleep. He kept wondering how all of this had happened, but maybe it didn't really matter at this point. His first mystery was solved—now he—and everyone—knew who killed Millicent Paulson.

PART II

It was April, and spring had finally arrived, at least temporarily, in Farmerton. It was none too soon. It had been a miserable winter in every way possible—record cold, record snowfall, and a murder-suicide to top it all off.

St. John's was reeling. An interim pastor had been sent from the church office who had experience working with congregations going through tough losses, but even this experienced woman had her work cut out for her. Usually, she came in after cases of sexual misconduct and subsequent removal of a pastor. This time, she was dealing with a pastor who murdered his choir director and later committed suicide. Still, Pastor Kate was doing an admirable job helping the congregants (at least those who were left) slowly pick up the pieces. She was a strong leader, with a kind and caring heart.

Some people, however, could not come to grips with what had transpired, and had completely left the church. Among the dispersed was Margaret Miller, the church secretary of twenty-five years. Margaret easily got a position working for a local company in their office. She wanted nothing to do with the church—not St. John's or any church—at that point in time. She had felt utterly betrayed by someone she had admired (and secretly loved) for years. It would a very long time before she would venture into a church again.

The choir was also dismantled. Edward provided special music from time to time and he was now the sole church musician. He was thrilled with the situation, as he had complete control over the music for each week. Pastor Kate gave him a lot more leeway than Pastor Michael or Millicent ever had. He was in music heaven.

Evelyn Russo had resigned the day after the pastor's

suicide, and gave notice to the school district that she would be departing after the school year. She didn't know where she would teach the next fall, but it wouldn't be in Farmerton, even though her beloved Millicent was buried in the churchyard. Evelyn often went to Millie's grave after dark and put a single rose on top of it when no one else was around. Anyone who saw the rose the next day assumed Charles left it there. Otherwise, she went to work and home, and that was it. She wanted nothing else to do with Farmerton.

Jared started taking Sunday shifts to make more money to pay for his brand new truck. He had never given away the stolen money as planned. He had thought about it a few times, and always chickened out. And after Pastor Michael's death, he decided not to give any of it away. His reasoning was if a pastor could kill someone and then kill himself, what was stealing a couple thousand dollars in comparison? So, Jared bought his brand new black Chevy Silverado Trail Boss 4 x 4 with all the bells and whistles, and never looked back. Working on Sunday mornings made it a lot easier to forget how he had amassed the down payment.

Donald Tripp had his own take on the Pastor Michael and Millicent ordeal. Having been spurned by Millicent when he propositioned her, he thought perhaps the pastor had experienced a similar humiliation. Maybe he couldn't handle the rejection as well as Donald had—well, had eventually. Donald had been pretty angry with Millicent for months, but he eventually got over it. Besides, there were other fish in the ocean, and currently he had his eye on a brand new one—Diane, the pastor's widow. He would give her another month or two, and then he'd make his move.

Simon's drinking had spiraled out of control after the deaths in the church. He just couldn't seem to pull himself out of it this time, so his sister had warily invited him to move in with her and her family for a while, providing he went to regular AA meetings and found a sponsor. Surprisingly, he took her up on it. It would be a long road ahead, but he felt he was on the right path for the first time in a long time.

Then there was Janie. Janie was on a mission—named Charles Paulson. Every move she made revolved around him. She knew what day and time Charles usually shopped at "the Pig," and made that her usually grocery shopping time, too. She still went to church because Charles still went to church. She despised the early service, but it was one he always attended. Soon it would be summer and they would only have one worship time a bit later in the morning—in between the usual times for both services, thank goodness. Some people were talking about having only one service sooner than that, as so many had left the congregation. Janie was one of those people who wanted this change, and the sooner, the better.

She also joined Charles' fitness club and conveniently worked out at the same time as he did at least once a week. Janie invested in some shapely workout ensembles and enjoyed the reactions of the males in the club when she pranced by them. They all seemed impressed—everyone, except Charles.

Janie even started cooking and baking more, two things she loathed even more than getting up early in the morning. She knew that Millicent had been excellent at both, as evidenced by parties like the one she had hosted the night she died. It had been fabulous. Janie thought she had better know how to cook at least a few things if she were ever to have a chance with Charles. She started watching food shows on television and looked up recipes and tips online constantly. She decided she would drop by the farmhouse one night after she had mastered a dish. Charles was most likely missing Millicent's good cooking, and she hoped to take advantage of the situation.

Gordon Roth was rather enjoying the fact that the Paulson name was now linked synonymously with scandal. He thought it couldn't happen to a better person than Charles Paulson, who always acted so arrogantly and, frankly, like his crap didn't stink. Gordon continued to go to church each Sunday. He liked Pastor Kate, but even better than listening to her sermons was watching Charles Paulson eat humble pie. Charles seemed to have a bit of the wind taken out of his sails, and Gordon loved all the speculations about why the Pastor might have killed Millicent. Every time Charles' name came up in a conversation, the question came up, and it delighted Gordon to no end. Gordon wondered why Charles even attended church, as the room became silent whenever he entered and buzzed with whispers after he left.

Diane still went to church every week, even though it was difficult for her. St. John's had been her family's church for many generations. Her descendants were buried in the church cemetery, and she now planned to be buried there one day, too, as she bought a new plot next to the ones owned by her parents.

Tax season was ramping up to a frenzy and she was grateful for the distraction and the extra income. She thought she might work full time after April, or possibly start her own accounting firm. She had made the decision—she was going to stay in Farmerton. Diane would, however, have to move out of the parsonage. The congregation had been gracious and gave her until the end of July to find a new home. She began looking for a house, but decided that instead, she would add on to a cabin she and Michael owned in the country.

Diane and Michael had bought fifteen acres of wooded land during the Great Recession and had built a rustic cabin on it. Diane had wanted to buy a cabin up north, closer to where her parents had retired, but she could never get Michael to take any real time off. When it was clear he would not go for that plan, she came up with the idea of owning a getaway right where they were. Over the years, they had added indoor plumbing and electricity, and a church member had built a huge stone fireplace for them. She would have another bedroom for guests added within the year. At present, there was a good-sized owners' suite which she and Michael had used, and a smaller bedroom and three-quarter bath, primarily used by Addie.

Michael and she had worked hard clearing hiking trails, and there was a small creek running through the property at which Michael occasionally fished. It was a great place for Michael to have a short "sabbath," or even for a few hours break when work seemed overwhelming. Diane loved to go there after her busy season was over. She wasn't about to let all their hard work go to waste. She could have moved immediately from the parsonage, but didn't feel like she was quite ready for that. She also didn't think Addie was quite ready for that, either.

It took quite a bit of convincing to get Addie back to

college after Michael's death. Fortunately, Addie's school—Diane and Michael's alma mater—was a very caring community. With the help of Addie's advisor, the resident assistant at her dorm, friends, and even a few professors, Addie decided to stick it out and finish the year so she didn't fall behind her class.

In June, Addie would be off as a camp counselor at the Bible Camp she had attended as a youth, and she couldn't wait to get there. It was her "happy place," and where she always found peace—and she needed peace, big time. She would come home to the family cabin, which would be their new home, for a week or two between the end of camp and the start of fall classes. It was a reasonable plan—at least Diane thought so, considering what Addie had been through. She prayed her daughter would be okay in the long run.

***

Charles traveled more and more for work these days. He had asked for this, in actuality. He wanted to keep a low profile in Farmerton. It was times like this that when living in a small town where everyone knows you, your family, and your story was not necessarily a positive thing. Charles believed working as much as possible, traveling the Midwest and sometimes the East Coast or the South, would be a wise choice.

When he was home, he worked out at his fitness club, although he was in the process of remodeling one of the bedrooms at the farmhouse into a workout room, and investigating whether or not his internet was strong enough for an exercise bike with programming. He was tired of the stares of people in public settings, and even more tired of Janie Johnson. She seemed to be everywhere he was. He was beginning to feel stalked. After his workout room was finished, he wouldn't have to put up with her as often—just Sunday mornings at church. He still went to St. John's. People often wondered why, but he had his reasons. He just wasn't interested in sharing them with anyone.

So it seemed that the members of the choir, those left at the church, and most of the residents of Farmerton were slowly moving on with their lives after the craziness of the past few months—everyone, that is, except Sgt. Joe Zimmerman.

***

Joe buckled his brand new belt. He had run out of room to punch holes in the previous one. He stared at himself in the mirror. He barely recognized the person looking back at him, which made him very happy. Between his new haircut—he'd gone back to Sissy's again for a trim—his current loss of twenty-five pounds to date, and his increased muscle tone, he looked like a different man—and that was a good thing in Joe's book.

He hadn't been at this weight since his early twenties. He felt great, but still planned to lose another five to ten pounds before it was all said and done. He had ordered two new summer uniforms, which was exciting. One was provided by the department, the other one he had to pay for out of his own pocket, which hurt a bit. He made sure to keep his receipts for taxes—Diane had given him that tip.

Diane. He had seen her often in the past couple of months. He didn't want to be a pest, but he still wanted to know why Pastor Michael would have killed Millicent Paulson, so he kept asking questions. Something about the entire scenario seemed off, yet at every turn, he ran into a dead end.

The coroner's report had come back and Pastor Michael's death had indeed been ruled a suicide. And even more damning, the tie he had hung himself with had fibers that perfectly matched those found on Millicent's neck, indicating he used the same red and blue tie to kill her.

Pastor Michael was also found to have a very high level of alcohol in his system, which seemed strange for the time of day, but Joe supposed that if one was planning to kill oneself, one might need more than a few drinks in order to go through with it. Still, it just seemed out of character, and Joe had a strange feeling about it in his gut (what was left of it, anyway.) But his lieutenant warned him about wasting so much time on a closed case, and he didn't want to do anything to jeopardize his career. For all the ups and downs, he still loved his work, and for all its positives and negatives, he still loved Farmerton.

***

By the end of April, Donald Tripp couldn't wait any longer and decided it was time to begin making his move on Diane. He was a shrewd businessman, so he decided he would begin by making a grand donation to the quilters at church. They were always complaining about the ancient sewing machine they used, so he bought them a new one—a very nice one—and donated some quilting supplies as well. The quilters were ecstatic and thought Donald was the nicest man on earth. Of course, he came to their next morning session to see how everyone liked his donations, and to make sure Diane knew what he had done.

After he left, a woman named Jennifer was what Diane's mother would have called "swooning" over Donald.

"Isn't he just the most amazing man?" she asked dreamily. "And so handsome, too!"

All the women nodded except Diane. She was not a Donald Tripp fan. Yes, it was nice that he had bought a much-needed machine for the group, but she knew that Donald always seemed to have a motive whenever he donated or did something. Someone had recently mentioned that he was considering running for mayor, and she thought perhaps that might be part of his current reason to impress. And it was no secret that he was a "ladies man" and had successfully enjoyed the company of many women in the area, something Diane truly did not understand at all. He certainly was not her type —not even close.

The donation was only the beginning of Donald's plan to interest Diane, though. Donald made sure to be at church every week, but until now had kept his distance. The quilt donation, however, gave him a segue into a conversation with Diane the following Sunday.

"How did the machine work for you ladies?" Donald asked.

Diane loathed the term "ladies," and tried not to roll her eyes. "I'm not one of those who uses the machine, but the women who do were thrilled. Thank you for your generous gift," Diane said.

Donald slicked his hair back with his hand—another thing Diane couldn't stand. It actually made her want to run away. Diane was about to turn to leave the area when he started talking again. Donald held up his empty coffee cup. "I'm going to get another one. May I get you a refill?" he asked in a sugary-sweet manner, stepping closer to her and looking her square in the eyes.

"No, thank you. I was just about to leave," she answered.

Donald was not one who enjoyed hearing the word "no," so he tried again.

"Oh, come on," he said, "you know you want it."

His suggestive language was not lost on Diane. She wondered how so many women could fall for this pile of manure talk.

"No, Donald," she said, and took a step back. She turned to leave, and Donald stepped in front of her, cutting her off. Diane's face took on a look that was a cross between anger and fear.

Just then, Joe, who had been watching the encounter from across the room for the past few minutes, stepped in.

"There you are, Diane," he said. "I wanted to talk to you, if you have a moment."

Diane looked relieved, and Donald finally backed off, his face turning crimson—not because of embarrassment, but rather from the fury rising inside his egotistical heart.

Joe walked with Diane to the door and opened it for her. Once outside, she turned to him.

"You needed to speak with me?" she asked Joe.

"Nah—not really, but it seemed like maybe Donald was bothering you and I thought you might like a diversion. I'm sorry if I was wrong and interrupted."

"It was a welcome interruption. Thank you, Joe," she said, looking up into his eyes and smiling. "That was very intuitive of you," she continued, "and I appreciate it."

Being so close to Diane and having her compliment him and smile at him was almost too much for Joe, and he had to step back slightly. "Comes with the job, I guess," he said finally.

She nodded in understanding. "Well, thank you again," she said.

"My pleasure," he said sincerely.

"Enjoy the rest of your day," Diane said, then turned to go to her car.

"Sure will. You, too," he said, thinking it was already the best day he'd had in a long time.

Joe watched Diane walk to her vehicle and drive away before moving a muscle. He didn't trust Donald Tripp. He wanted to make certain he wouldn't try to catch her in the parking lot and continue his pursuit of her. Joe thought the man had no tact, and not much in the way of morals, either. Joe knew he was no saint himself, but next to Donald, he felt almost angelic.

After Diane's car turned the corner, Joe walked back inside the church building. He passed Oscar, the custodian, who was putting the bulletins which had been left behind in the pews into the recycling bin, grumbling to himself, which seemed to be his usual demeanor.

Joe had seen Oscar smile more lately, however. He seemed the least affected of all the choir members, staff, and parishioners by the two unexpected deaths in the parish. In fact, they seemed to have an almost positive effect on him. Oscar had just been given a raise. Now that there was only one musician to pay, Oscar had petitioned for a salary increase at the last council meeting and had received it. Even though people didn't like his surliness, they did know he did a good job cleaning the church and that he would be difficult to replace. The church council was afraid he would quit if he didn't get the raise, and that one more loss would be the very last thing the congregation needed at the time. They unanimously gave him his request, which resulted in a significant bump in wages, effective immediately.

Joe rounded the corner to get his jacket when he happened past Donald Tripp. Donald was now surrounded by a small group of women of various ages, who were fawning over him as he soaked up their adulation. Joe just didn't understand it. Maybe he just didn't understand women in general, he thought to himself. He wondered why men like Donald could have anyone—well, almost anyone—he wanted.

And it still puzzled him how someone like Charles Paulson had been married to such a kind and beautiful woman like Millicent, or even why Janie Johnson was after Charles now. The women at the beauty salon were all talking about how Janie was practically stalking Charles. He didn't see what women saw in either Donald or Charles, and he doubted he ever would.

Joe grabbed his jacket and left. Once in his car, he sat there for a few minutes, thinking about his earlier discussion with Diane in this same parking lot. Those kind words of hers. Those eyes of hers. He felt like she could melt him with them. Joe shook off the thoughts and decided to go home and go for a run. He'd been doing that the past week since most of the snow had finally disappeared from the road. He needed to work off some steam—literally.

***

Two Sundays later, Janie Johnson cornered Charles Paulson in the choir room of the church. Charles had gone there to retrieve some of Millicent's personal items Oscar had found while spring cleaning. There was a small box with a hairbrush and comb, a music book, and a notebook filled with song suggestions for church services mapped out for months in advance. There was also a Christmas card. Just as Charles began reading the card, the door to the choir room opened. There were no other entrances or exits, so Charles had nowhere to run to when Janie intruded.

"There you are," she said, throwing back her hair, a seductive smile crossing her lips. Janie was as thrilled as a cat who had just cornered a mouse.

Charles closed the Christmas card quickly and looked at her somberly. "Janie," he said, acknowledging her presence, but nothing more.

"You're a tough one to catch," she said, moving uncomfortably close to Charles.

He stepped back, ignoring her comment. "I was just picking up a few of Millicent's belongings," he said, putting the card he had been reading into the box in his other hand.

Janie tried another tactic. "I'm so sorry, Charles. She was way too young to die. I just can't figure out why Pastor Michael would kill her. Maybe he was interested in her and she said no, so he killed her."

Charles couldn't help thinking at that moment that he

wished Janie would fall off the edge of the earth.

"You're talking about our pastor, Janie—and my wife!" he said, sounding offended. Then he began to worry she would begin spreading this theory all over town.

Janie, not wanting to put Charles off, softened her tone. "I guess you're right. But it just doesn't make any sense."

Charles began to get teary. "Many things in life don't make any sense, Janie. You should know that—losing your own husband way too early," he said.

"Yes," she said. She couldn't tell Charles that she rarely even thought about her late husband, with him seeming so full of grief at the moment, so that was the best response she could give him.

She truly felt bad for Charles and put her hand on his shoulder. To her surprise, this time he didn't step back. Instead, he moved in and kissed her gently on the lips. She was stunned. Her dreams were finally coming true. Not wanting to blow it, she didn't say anything to him after they parted.

"I'm so sorry," Charles said. "I just got carried away. Forgive me," he said again in a gentlemanly way.

"No need to apologize. Would you like to have dinner together tonight? If you don't want to be out in public yet, I could cook for you at my home—or at yours," Janie suggested.

"Your place would be lovely," he said.

Janie loved it when he spoke like that. "How about six?" she asked.

"Perfect," he said.

"I'll see you then," Janie said and turned to leave, beaming with happiness.

After the door closed to the choir room behind her, Charles let out a disgusted sigh and put down the box. He pulled out the Christmas card and read it once more. It wasn't signed, but it read: *Millie — I hope you know how special you are.*

Charles was quite sure he knew its author. That's why he reacted as he did when Janie suggested the pastor might have been sweet on Millicent. That's the only reason he had done what he had done—the kiss, and accepting the dinner invitation. He would do anything to keep Janie from talking all over town.

Charles' hands were trembling as he put the card into the box, then headed straight home. The first thing he did when he arrived at the farm was throw the entire box into the old oil drum turned burn barrel, and lit a match. He stared at the flames until he was certain the box, and especially the card, were incinerated. Then he pulled out his cell phone and made a call.

***

Later that afternoon, Joe's phone rang and Diane's name flashed at him. His heart started beating harder, and he hoped that she was not in any sort of trouble. The last time he saw that name on his phone was the day that Pastor Michael had killed himself. His mind went quickly to Donald Tripp and the events of the morning, and hoped the man wasn't bothering Diane again—or worse.

Joe didn't even say hello when he answered. "Diane! Is everything okay?" He was practically shouting into the phone.

Diane chuckled a bit on the other end of the line, and

Joe began to relax.

"Everything is fine, Joe," she said. "Thanks to you," she added, "but thank you for your concern."

"That's good to hear," he said with a sigh of relief.

"I've been thinking about this morning," Diane continued. "You really helped me out of a precarious situation," she said seriously. "I feel I owe you a dinner. Care to join me this evening?"

Joe almost dropped his phone.

"You don't owe me a thing, but dinner sounds awesome. What time?"

"How about six? Do you have any food restrictions?"

He wanted to say, *Do I look like someone who has food restrictions?* but thought better of it. "Not really. I'm not much on seafood, but I like pretty much everything else." Joe wished he hadn't said that about seafood. He didn't want to sound like a food prude. He just hadn't acquired much of a taste for that type of food growing up in his house, or his grandma's. It was strictly meat and potatoes at both homes. If he ate anything that came out of the water, it was at a Friday night fish fry, or whatever his Grandpa brought home from his fishing trips when Joe was a little boy. But for Diane, he would eat squid or octopus—even if the thought of it nauseated him.

"I'll see you at six, Joe," Diane said.

"Sure thing," Joe said, and hit the end-call button.

He stared at his phone for a few minutes. He actually went to his phone app to make sure he had truly received a call from Diane and that he wasn't hallucinating. But there it was—proof right on his phone. He smiled, and then panicked. What was he going to wear? He only had one nice shirt that still fit him reasonably, and he had worn it the past two Sundays to church, including that morning.

Joe searched his closet, to no avail, then looked at the clock. He still had time to drive to Madison and go to a store. The one shop in Farmerton that sold clothing was closed on Sundays, so he didn't really have another option. It had been inevitable that he would have to update his wardrobe at some point, but he had been trying to hold on until he got to his final target weight, but this was Diane he was talking about. It wasn't every day he was asked to someone's home for dinner, and for that someone to be Diane—well, it was a miracle. So Joe hopped in his car and off he went, glad that he had gotten his run in earlier.

***

Janie met Charles at the door with a smile on her face and a glass of wine in her hand. She wore a tight, white V-neck sweater and black slacks, which accentuated her curves. Earrings dangled from her earlobes and Charles caught a whiff of perfume. It was a French designer scent—at least she had good taste in that area.

Charles' first instinct was to turn right around, but that wouldn't be very nice. It was too over the top for him—too much, too soon—but he should have expected this considering it was Janie.

Janie seemed to pick up on his reaction and backed up a step or two. "Come in," she said. "Can I get you some wine, or something else?"

Charles thought he might need a glass of wine to get through the evening, so he agreed to a glass of Chardonnay.

He came into the house, a one-year-old home on the edge of town. It was a mostly open design, with the living room, dining area, and kitchen all within view of one another. The only thing that divided the space was a bioethanol fireplace of impressive design. The modern design, with a kitchen with white quartz countertops and gray cabinetry, and a living area with complementary furniture, looked like something out of a magazine. Simply put, Janie's house was gorgeous. Once more, Charles was surprised. The home looked out of place in Farmerton—it was more like a house he would have seen back in Naperville. Then, again, Janie had moved back to town from Illinois.

As impressive as the house was, Janie apologized ahead of time for the simple meal. Even though she had been working on her cooking and baking, and she planned to take cooking classes in the summer, for now, he would have to put up with her best "go-to" dish—chicken noodle casserole.

Charles had to admit the food was quite palatable. Janie served a salad on the side of her main dish with a homemade dressing, made buttermilk biscuits by scratch, and scooped vanilla ice cream over the brownies she had baked for dessert. She had only hours to prepare for this, so it was almost as impressive as her home.

Charles asked her more about her move back to Farmerton. She mentioned her husband's unexpected death and her dad's health issues. Then she apologized and said, "Of course, it's nothing like what you are going through, Charles." When she said that, she gently put her hand on his, but after seeing his reaction, she quickly removed it.

"I'm not so certain about that, Janie. It must have been quite a shock to you when your husband died while at work."

"It was at the time, for sure," she said. Janie didn't want to mention that she hadn't truly been in love with her husband at the time of his death—if ever. Charles would think she was a horrible person if she even hinted at something like that. She often felt guilty about her feelings, but she couldn't change the truth—that her heart had always belonged to Charles.

He looked at her with those pale blue eyes and she almost melted. "You're too kind, Charles," she said softly.

They chatted about their exercise workout routines and Charles' new fitness room in his home, which was almost completed. His new stationary cycle would be arriving within a week, and he could begin his cycling program.

Janie felt relieved when she learned about his new workout room. She had thought Charles had been avoiding her by not attending the fitness club. Now she understood why he hadn't been around much lately.

They finished dessert and talked for a while longer, then Charles took the napkin from his lap and set it next to his plate. "Well, my apologies, Janie, but I have a very early morning meeting tomorrow, then I'm off on a business trip for the remainder of the week. This was a lovely evening, Janie, and I truly appreciate the meal."

Janie was going out of her mind. Charles was complimenting her and thanking her. She was disappointed to hear he would be gone so long, but she could wait. She'd been waiting for Charles for years. Everything was finally falling into place. All her efforts of the past had been worth it.

Janie saw Charles to the foyer. She hesitated at the

door before opening it, but when Charles looked disinterested, she reluctantly opened the door for him and they said good night. Charles thanked her once more, but that was all. Janie had wanted another kiss so badly and had thought about initiating one, but she knew that if she pushed him too soon, she might blow it for good, so she held back. She would kiss Charles Paulson another time, and she'd be sure he never forgot it when she did.

Charles drove away, thankful that the evening had been far more tolerable than he had imagined it would be—then again, he had had fairly low expectations. He had been impressed with Janie's home, her casserole was good comfort food, and there had even been some reasonable conversation. All in all, it had been a successful evening.

After he turned the corner, he pulled over and took out his cell phone. He texted a number, and shortly after, his phone rang. He answered on his device, hating how the car speaker could be heard by anyone within a reasonable distance.

"How did it go?" He waited for an answer. "Same here. I'll see you tomorrow. Good night."

***

Joe was in such a daze when he left Diane's, he almost missed the vehicle creeping up the lane from the church cemetery. It was dark and he wondered why anyone would be in the cemetery this late in the evening. He pulled his car over and watched for a moment. To his surprise, instead of heading out of the church parking lot, the car stopped near the back door and a person got out. He couldn't really tell who it was at the beginning. He thought it was a female, but she was tall. They wore all black, donned in a knee-length raincoat with the hood up. The church had some lighting in the back, which he thought they'd better upgrade in the future, as he could barely see what was happening.

The person turned their head left, then right, and proceeded to the door, which had a combination lock on it. The church council had gotten tired of handing out key after key to members who needed to get into the church, so they finally put this type of combination lock on the back door only.

The person opened the door and went inside, but never turned on a light. That made Joe even more suspicious, so he drove into the lot and parked near the dark-colored sedan. He wished so badly that he had his cruiser so he could run the license plate. Instead, he called the office and had them do it. They would text him when they had the information. Joe walked to the door and waited while the computer was doing its work.

He checked the windows on the door, then a few nearby, and saw no one. He went back to the door again, not wanting to miss the person when they came out. Just then his phone pinged.

The car was registered to one Evelyn Marie Russo. At least now he knew who he was dealing with as he waited for her to emerge from the building. He wondered what she was doing here now that she no longer worked at the church. He stepped to the side of the door, watching it closely. Finally, after fifteen minutes, she came out.

She saw his car, then looked around and saw him standing nearby and jumped a bit, dropping some of the papers in her hands.

"I'm sorry," Joe said. "I didn't mean to scare you. Officer Joe Zimmerman here," he added, just so she wouldn't completely freak out on him, especially since he was out of uniform. He bent over and helped her pick up a sheet of paper, glancing briefly at it.

"I...I...just had to pick up some music I forgot at the church," she said.

Of course, that made some sense, although she could have done that anytime. Going into a dark building after hours, not using any lights, seemed a bit strange to him—although as more than one person had pointed out—Evelyn was an unusual person.

There wasn't really anything Joe could charge Evelyn with. She hadn't technically broken into the church. He had no reason to doubt her about the music, especially as he saw what looked like music on the page he had picked up from the ground. He didn't read music, but he had been going to church lately, and saw music written out on the pages of the hymnal each week. So Joe just told her to be careful, as someone might mistake her for a thief and she could get hurt.

Evelyn looked mortified at that, thanked him, and hurried to her car. He watched her drive off, thinking about what a day it had been.

Hours later, Joe laid wide-eyed in his bed, still going over the events of the day. It had all begun at church. He'd been going almost every week for a while now, and surprisingly found himself enjoying it. He thought Pastor Kate was easier to understand than any other pastor he had ever heard preach. She didn't use lofty words, but had a way of connecting the readings to illustrations from real life, and he appreciated it.

Then there had been the coffee hour afterward, and the encounter with Diane and Donald Tripp. He thought again about the man's aggressive behavior toward Diane and it made him angry. No woman ever deserved that type of treatment, but he especially felt it was awful when it was on top of a loss like Diane had recently endured.

Yet he felt a bit two-faced about blaming Donald, because he too thought of little else than Diane these days—and nights. Especially this night. Joe just couldn't get over the unexpected invitation to her home and the meal she had cooked for him. She had made beef tips served over his choice of rice or noodles, or both. They were the most flavorful and tender tips he had ever had. Diane had credited the local beef she bought every year from an area farmer.

They had talked about high school, then about how their lives had—or hadn't—turned out as expected. Diane mentioned again that while she was excited to go to college at first, and everyone else had great expectations for her, deep down she had always wanted to get married and start a family. She also loved the idea of marrying a pastor. Her favorite aunt, who was also her godmother, had married a member of the clergy. Diane had always admired their life together, and all the activities their entire family was involved in at their church in another part of the state. So, when she met this handsome soccer player, who was accepted to a seminary, it was a done deal.

Joe talked about what led him to law enforcement, crediting the police liaison who dropped in at the schools from time to time or presented special programs to the students. He had always looked up to the officer, and in high school started talking to him more about his job. He was a Farmerton City Police Department officer. Going to the schools was only a fraction of his work, although the officer's favorite.

Joe was used to having his classmates and many younger kids in town look up to him as an athlete, and while he was a very good one, he knew he wasn't a D-1 recruit, and that would have been the only way he would have gone to college. He just didn't like schoolwork very much. He liked action and getting out and about. He liked helping people. He enjoyed meeting people in the community. He even liked working the county fair, an event some officers disliked.

Diane had been impressed when he told her about his reasons for choosing law enforcement. "Joe," she had said, "you have a servant's heart."

If anyone else would have said something like that to him, he would have run for the hills, or perhaps laughed at them, but when those words came out of Diane's mouth, it made him feel special and appreciated. It made him feel good about himself in a way he had never felt before. For all the glory and praise Joe had received as an athlete, and even his promotions at work, he still had less than stellar self-esteem, and it had been at an all-time low since his divorce from Stacy. That was part of the reason he had become such a lump and stayed one over the years. But now, that was changing.

Diane had complimented Joe on this appearance. He had gone to one of the last department stores in the city, and had a salesperson help him select some new clothes. The woman was very professional and said she had been working there for a long time and boldly mentioned that she was good at her job. According to Diane, she had been correct. She told him that he looked like a "new man."

So now it was midnight and he was wide awake, thinking about her. He felt so bad for her losing her husband like that. He still couldn't really believe it. He had thought it crazy enough when Millicent had been murdered, but then to find out that it was Pastor Michael was beyond craziness.

He thought about all those other people he had interviewed. Even though they had alibis, the thought of one of them being a murderer would have been easier to swallow. People like that womanizing Donald Tripp, or Janie, relentlessly chasing after Charles Paulson. Or that surly Oscar the custodian, the strange duck Evelyn Russo, or an angry Roth with an old grudge. Any of them would be easier to understand than Pastor Michael.

He decided he had to drop these thoughts from his mind. He had to begin a shift at seven A.M. Joe finally managed to shut his mind off for a moment, and was out like a light.

***

The next Sunday at church, Joe was approached during coffee hour by an older member of the congregation, a gentleman named Edner. He didn't know how old Edner was, but he remembered thinking Edner was old back when he was a kid and had gone to services with his grandma.

"Joseph," Edner began, calling him by the name his grandmother always used for him.

"I'm wondering if you would consider taking on the task of collection counter with me? It's not very difficult. I had a young man helping me for the past year or so—Jared—but now he is more interested in making money than counting it, and riding around in his fancy new pickup truck."

Now Joe was beginning to enjoy church, but he wasn't ready to take on duties—especially weekly ones. He made the excuse that he never knew when he might be called to duty, which wasn't a complete lie, and that he sometimes worked weekends—again, truth.

Edner sighed. "Very well. Let me know if you change your mind. We like to have two counters, you know, to keep one honest," he said so seriously that Joe almost laughed. Instead, Joe nodded his head, thinking that no one would steal from a church—would they? But then again, he went back to his usual mantra—that he had seen enough things to know that anything is possible.

He thought about Jared. He was one of the choir members, too, and Joe had noticed that he was nowhere to be found on Sundays as of late. So many of the choir members had vanished—Evelyn, Margaret, Jared, Pastor Michael, and Simon. Joe hadn't thought about Simon in quite a while. The last he had heard, he was going to move in with his sister, but he didn't know if that had happened or not.

Edner had gone back to his counting duties once he had refilled his cup of coffee. Joe took his coffee and moved to a small, round high table in the room. He looked around, hoping to see Diane. He saw Donald Tripp out of the corner of his eye, talking again to a few women. Joe didn't think he ever saw Donald talking with men. He was probably hanging out in hopes of running into Diane. Again, Joe felt a pang of guilt, as he was doing the exact same thing.

Finally, Diane appeared, walking with Pastor Kate toward the coffee pot. They were in a discussion, yet Diane looked his way and gave him a smile. Just to make sure it was for him, he looked around. There wasn't anyone else close to him, so he was happy that he had smiled back.

He didn't want to be too forward, so he waited to see what would happen. The pastor and Diane got coffee, then Pastor Kate began making her rounds to various members around the room. Diane, to Joe's delight, came over to talk to him. Joe's heart was beating so hard he thought perhaps the others in the room could hear it.

He was wearing another one of his new shirts today, and Diane complimented him on it. He would have to go back to the same store and see if he could find that clerk and thank her for her advice. Maybe he'd even get another shirt. He wanted to give it a few more weeks, though, as he was still going down in weight. He had almost achieved his target goal.

"Officer," Diane said playfully, with a smile.

Joe could hardly answer. "Diane," he said, almost like he couldn't believe she was actually speaking to him.

Joe had thought of little else but Diane for an entire week now. He even started to forget about all the events of the past months. It was the beginning of May. The snow was gone. The sun was out. There was green grass. Most of the trees had new, bright green leaves, and the late-bloomers had buds. There were even a few varieties of flowers beginning to blossom. He had always heard that springtime was a time for falling in love, and at that moment, he felt like he might truly be in love—possibly for the first time in his life. The thought was almost too scary, as he didn't have a great track record in that arena. The near-empty coffee cup in his hand began shaking, so he quickly tossed it in a nearby wastebasket.

When he turned around, Diane was so close to him that he almost felt faint.

"Walk me to my car?"

"Sure thing," Joe answered, wishing he was better with words.

Diane threw her paper cup away, and together they started for the parking lot. Donald Tripp was watching the entire encounter, his face turning red again, a vein popping in his temple.

Once they were outside, Joe was about to ask Diane if she would like to join him for lunch or dinner, when she mentioned she was meeting her parents and daughter for a lunch in Iowa. He was disappointed, but did his best not to show it.

Diane hopped in her car and was off, Joe watching as she drove away. He stood there for a few minutes, thinking. He concluded that he was going to come up with some ideas for a date, then work up the nerve to ask Diane out. He was a grown man, after all, even if she did make him feel like a giddy teenager in some ways. "Life is short," his grandmother used to tell him, one of her many wise sayings. He decided he needed to get on this before he lost his chance—or his nerve.

***

Over the next month, Farmerton was the quietest it had been in months. It almost felt the same as it had pre-murder and suicide to Joe—that is, until the first week of

June. Then things got more interesting again. There was nothing as major as the Paulson/Pastor fiasco, but the events made Joe start to wonder again.

It all began with a simple traffic stop. It was a warm, sunny Friday afternoon when a huge, black pickup truck blew past the spot Joe had parked to have lunch. He had his radar on just in case, but doubted anyone would be on the road at this time of day. Most were at work in town or in the fields or pastures mending fences, although he should have remembered that the factory day shift let out at two.

Joe had just been ready to pour a cup of coffee and have a sandwich. He threw down the plastic cup that came with the thermos, then flipped on his lights and sirens and screeched out onto the roadway after the speeder, letting out an expletive on the way. He was hungry. It was just after two and he hadn't had a chance to eat lunch yet.

Jared groaned when he heard the siren and saw the red and blue flashing lights behind him, but knew he had to stop. He pulled over onto the gravel shoulder. He had been in a hurry to go fishing after his shift. It was such a beautiful day, so he was heading out to the trout streams west of town. He hadn't been paying attention to his speed. He just knew he had to get outside after being inside the dark factory all day—his least favorite part of his job.

Joe pulled up behind the truck, a bit to its left side. He got out of the cruiser, put on his hat, and walked to the driver's window, his hand near his weapon. Traffic stops were the second most dangerous police actions next to answering domestic violence calls, so he was prepared.

As he neared the vehicle, he could see a bit of the head

of the person and it seemed familiar to him. So he wasn't surprised when it was someone he knew—sort of—one of the former choir members he had interviewed, Jared. Now he saw the vehicle to which Edner had referred at church. It was a beast—and beautiful. *How could this kid afford this?* he wondered.

"Jared, right?" Joe asked.

"Yes, sir," said Jared, hoping that if he was polite he might only get a warning.

"What's the hurry?" Joe asked.

Jared told him about his plans to trout fish. He was in a hurry to get there and enjoy some of the sunshine.

Joe could empathize. He couldn't wait to get done with his shift at three, and hoped his paperwork wouldn't delay his time on the job too much. He told him to stay put and he'd be right back. He went and entered the plates and got his report. Jared had a pretty clean driving record for someone his age, just one ticket four years before. Joe decided to let him off with a warning and walked back to the truck.

"Jared, next time slow down. You want to make sure to *get* to your fishing spot. Better late than never." That was a line Joe often used with speeders.

Joe held the warning in his hand and thought again about the truck, which made him think again about Edner. He started to hand the sheet of paper to Jared and Jared started reaching out to take it.

"By the way, you are really missed at church, especially by Edner. He told me you used to help him with the offering counting..."

When Joe said this, Jared fumbled the paper and it fell to the ground. Thankfully, it wasn't windy, so Joe could easily pick it up.

He turned back to Jared and handed it to him again. Jared's face was as white as snow and his hand shook as he took the warning slip from the officer.

"He tried to get me to take over the duties, but I sometimes work on the weekends. He says they always have two people do it—to keep it honest."

Jared looked like he might get sick, so Joe asked, "Are you okay?"

"Yeah," Jared lied. "Just need to get out into some fresh air, I guess."

"Well, you have a good time fishing now. Don't make me regret not giving you a ticket," Joe said, watching Jared carefully.

"Yes, sir," Jared said, looking straight ahead, his hands clenched on the wheel so the officer wouldn't see them shaking.

"Have a good one," Joe said.

"Thanks, you too," he said, and started up his truck once again.

After Joe had returned to his cruiser, Jared finally let out the breath he had been holding. He sighed. He shouldn't have been speeding—it was too risky. Heck, he shouldn't have this truck in the first place, he thought. It's probably too risky, too. He turned back onto the road, using his turn signal, which he never would have done if a sheriff's officer wasn't right behind him. He made sure to slowly accelerate down the road, watching his speed like a hawk. He was still going to go fishing, but there was no way he was going to enjoy it the way he thought he would. At least he hadn't gotten a ticket. That would have taken a good chunk of his overtime pay, which he used to make his truck payments. Jared sighed as he drove to the stream, wishing he could go back in time. He never should have stolen from the church.

Joe watched Jared drive away. *What was that all about?* He remembered Jared being nervous around him during his interview after the murder, but this time he had seemed reasonably relaxed— until he had brought up the subjects of church and Edner. Maybe he would ask Edner more about Jared on Sunday, although he was a bit afraid that Edner would continue his quest to recruit him into counting duty. He decided he would talk to him if the occasion arose. Otherwise, he would just live with it. Still, there was something about the whole situation with Jared that just didn't feel right. So many things just didn't feel right, ever since Millie's death almost six months ago.

Joe made an executive decision right then. He wasn't going to ruin the rest of his day thinking about it. He had finished his report and it was just after three. He called in and checked out for the day and drove home. He planned to get a run in before supper. That always seemed to clear his mind and made him relax. It would be a perfect thing to do on this gorgeous day.

***

Joe was called into work the next Sunday, as the assigned officer was ill. So, it was another week after that until he was able to get back to church—and got to see Diane. He thought of little else than her, so he was excited when their paths crossed again that Sunday. He was just about to ask her out when Edner appeared to get another cup of coffee, and his mind flew back to his encounter with

Jared. Joe reluctantly excused himself and went to talk to him.

"How are you today, Edner?"

The older gentleman grumbled a bit. "I'd be better if I had some help. You haven't changed your mind, have you?"

"No, I'm sorry. As I said, I sometimes get called into duty on the weekends—in fact, that's why I wasn't here last Sunday," Joe added, happy to have proof to back up his excuse. "I did wonder, however, if you had a minute to discuss your former helper?"

"Very well, but I have to get back to my work. Follow me."

Joe followed Edner down the hallway. They stopped just outside the choir room, where the collection plates sat on a table nearby.

"Don't you worry about someone touching this while you're off to get coffee?" Joe asked Edner.

"Somewhat. I never had to worry about that when I had a helper. Jared used to watch it for me, or Harold before he died. Now I just hope and pray it's safe. There's usually no one down here after worship anymore—not since the choir disbanded. The only one who was usually around during this time, if there was anyone, was the choir director, God rest her soul."

Joe asked more about Jared, but Edner had nothing much to say. He said he was a quiet young man who did a good job helping him. Again, he mentioned he was sorry that Jared had chosen his factory work over the Lord's work, as he put it. Joe thanked him for his time, then hurried back to the fellowship area, hoping that Diane was still around.

She was still there, and smiled at him as he entered the room and he joined her at a high table.

"Did Edner finally convince you to help him?" Diane asked, chuckling.

"No. I truly can't commit to that. I just wanted to ask him about his former helper, Jared. You knew Jared from choir. Did you ever notice anything unusual about him, or did he have any problems with the choir director?"

Diane looked a bit shocked at the mention of the choir director. "Millicent? Why do you ask?"

"I don't know, really. I just know that he acted really nervous when I interviewed him after her death. Then, I saw him again not long ago, and he acted very upset when I mentioned church. So, it just got me thinking again."

Diane started looking poorly as he talked about the situation, and Joe noticed. Finally, she said quietly, "What's done, is done."

"I'm sorry, Diane. I shouldn't have brought up the subject. It must be hard for you to even hear about it." Joe wanted to crawl in a hole. He had fallen in love with this woman, and now he was causing her pain with the mention of an awful memory. He decided to change the subject.

"Want to get out of here? I could treat you to lunch somewhere? It doesn't have to be here in town—we could go somewhere else, or just pick something up and eat outside somewhere. It's another beautiful day."

Diane seemed to be regaining her composure, and nodded. She threw away her cup and napkin and together they walked to the parking lot.

She suggested going through a drive-through in a bigger town not far from Farmerton. They decided to eat their food on a picnic table near a river. Joe was out of his mind with happiness. The sun was shining. He was eating the best burger around—a great treat now that he didn't indulge in that type of thing often anymore. And best of all, he was with Diane. What else mattered?

They spent the entire afternoon together, much to Joe's delight. They walked on a small nature trail near the picnic area. They would have hiked, but they were both still in church clothes.

By the time he got home, it was almost suppertime. He would have a salad, he decided, after he went for a run. He needed to cancel out a few of the calories and fat from his splurge at lunch. Joe took off his dress clothes and changed into shorts and a T-shirt. This was much more his style, he thought to himself, although he certainly appreciated the response he repeatedly received to his new wardrobe— if one could call a few new shirts and pairs of pants a wardrobe. Joe put on his running shoes and hit the pavement, a huge smile on his face.

***

The smile stayed on his face for almost two weeks. Diane had called him the day after their lunch to thank him. The next Saturday, she invited him for coffee and fresh-baked coffee cake at her house.

Joe noticed a few boxes sitting in some of the rooms, and Diane noticed him eyeing them.

"They're for my move," she said.

Joe's countenance fell. *Diane was leaving!*

"I'm moving to our cabin out in the country. This house belongs to the church. They offered to sell it to me last week, but I need to get away from...certain memories," she said.

"That makes sense. I didn't know you had property," Joe said, gradually recovering his wits.

Diane told him the story about how they came to own land because she could never get Michael to take a real vacation. It was a compromise, to have somewhere to retreat from the pressures of everyday life. She mentioned they were into "staycations" before the term had even been coined.

She continued on about her plans to add on to her abode over time, but for now, it would be good enough for her, and for Addie during the brief times her daughter was actually home. She talked about Addie's summer job at the Bible Camp, and what a godsend it had been. Getting away and being with so many positive, loving people had done wonders for her only child.

The weeks had been so wonderful, Joe rarely gave Jared a second thought. And when he did think about him, he remembered Diane's words: "What's done, is done." She was right—it was time to move forward and forget the past. And he was all for the future—especially if Diane was going to be a part of it.

***

Joe was not happy when he had to work a three-to-eleven shift, but it was vacation season, and everyone had to pick up the slack. Joe thought about the fact that he hadn't taken a vacation in years. Part of that was financial, the other part was he just didn't have anyone to do things with. He thought that perhaps that might begin to change in the future, and started Googling best places for a vacation whenever he had an extra moment. Maybe by next summer, he would have a travel partner. He tried not to think about it too much, as if he was afraid he'd jinx it by thinking such thoughts.

Joe was thinking about places he liked to visit and was parked on the shoulder of a county highway when a car zig-zagged down the other side of the road heading his direction. It narrowly missed his vehicle and continued on its way. Joe pulled out quickly and did a U-turn, lights and siren blaring. The vehicle still didn't stop. It was as if it didn't see him at all.

Then he watched the car leave the road, head down into the ditch, and finally come to rest in a dense cornfield.

Joe radioed in for help, then proceeded to the car, which had rolled over on its top. He was shocked to see someone actually crawling out through the driver's window, blood streaming down the side of his face—yet, even more surprisingly, the man was singing.

"Ninety-nine bottles of beer on the wall," the man slurred, and then laughed. "Ouch—dammit! That hurt!"

"Hold still, buddy," Joe said as he approached the intoxicated man. Then he noticed who it was. It was Simon from the choir. He hadn't seen him in a while. People said that he had been at his sister's home and had been doing better. Obviously, that was over.

Simon looked at him, smiled, and then fell flat on his face. Joe checked to make sure he had a pulse and was still breathing. Thankfully, he was, as Joe hadn't been looking forward to resuscitating him if he hadn't been.

An ambulance and another officer arrived. The EMTs looked Simon over, then took him to the closest area hospital, as his wounds did not appear to be life-threatening. Joe went back to his cruiser and starting filling out a report, shaking his head in amazement. He would check on Simon after he had received treatment and had a chance to detoxify. That man was one lucky son-of-a-gun, Joe thought to himself as he typed in the details of the accident.

***

Simon's eyes were closed when Joe went into his darkened hospital room. Simon opened them when Joe opened the blinds a bit so he could write a few things down. Simon's eyes were bloodshot, with dark circles around them. He was hooked up to an IV and groaned at the light, trying to shield his eyes with his hand.

"What'd you do that for?" Simon asked, annoyed and squinting.

"I need to write down your statement. If you'd rather I put on that overhead light..."

"No!"

"Okay, then. So, what happened last night, Simon?"

"I guess I had a few too many," he said.

"That's an understatement. You were almost twice the legal limit. You're lucky to be alive, Simon."

"Maybe. Maybe I'd be better off dead."

"Why do you say that?" Joe inquired.

He didn't answer at first, but a tear rolled down his cheek. "I'm just no good," he said without elaborating.

"How so?"

"Living with my sister—like a little kid. No good as a developer, and now I can't even sell a house."

Joe knew the housing market wasn't great in their area, but he thought it had been picking up in the last month or so. Then again, looking at Simon, he understood why one might shy away from dealing with him. He didn't exactly demand respectability or confidence in his abilities. He was certain Simon was not the average person's first choice when looking for a realtor.

"Tried to sell the pastor's wife a house, but no—she's going to live at their cabin out near Paulson's. I thought maybe she'd change her mind when the parsonage went on the market—I was handling it for the church for half the normal percentage rate, and I would have given her a great deal—but no—not even then."

Joe hadn't known where Diane's property was located, and was a bit surprised that it was close to the Paulson's property. He wasn't surprised that Diane didn't want to live in the parsonage, though. If Simon had seen what he and Diane had seen on that staircase, he'd understand, but it wasn't Joe's place to share that information.

"I'm just no good," Simon reiterated.

"No, you're a good person, Simon. But you have a problem."

"You bet I do. If Paulson had sold me that land I wanted to develop years ago, I'd be just fine. I wouldn't be out trying to sell parsonages at half charge."

"I meant your drinking, Simon."

"Oh, yeah. That, too. Like I said, I'm no good."

Joe was getting nowhere, only going around in circles. He asked Simon a few more questions. He discovered that Simon had gotten drunk at his sister's after she and her family had gone away for the weekend and the sale of the parsonage had gone awry. At least there wasn't a tavern involved, where Joe'd had to go out and possibly fine or charge someone for letting Simon get so drunk and then drive.

Joe left the hospital, feeling sorry for Simon. He certainly was a mess right now, and Joe sincerely hoped he would get some treatment in the near future before something even worse happened to him—or someone else. There was a good chance some counseling may even be court-ordered, although he knew it would be much more effective if Simon admitted he had a problem and truly wanted help. It was good that Simon still had a support system, which it appeared he did. Joe had seen Simon's sister arriving at the hospital as he left. He believed that was a good sign, that she hadn't completely written him off after this slip-up. Joe got into his unit and decided to take a little trip out into the country. He told himself he was going there to patrol, but deep down, he was curious to see exactly where Diane's property was located, if he could find it. All his thoughts these days always came back to her.

***

Another week passed. Simon had been discharged from the hospital and voluntarily entered an AODA rehabilitation program, which would most likely be looked upon positively at his upcoming court appearance.

Joe was enjoying the summer weather and had gone on several hikes over the past few weeks and even a recent bike ride with Diane. He hadn't been on a bike in years, and decided he might get a stationary one before winter, so he would be sure to stay in shape, and maybe buy a used one next spring. He loved the way he looked and felt. He also loved the way the women down at Sissy's looked at him, too, even if the majority of them were old enough to be his mother, and the others already married.

He had just had a trim a few days ago. He decided it was worth the extra cost to go to Sissy's, just to know what was going on in town. He had thought the barbershop and Bud's had been good places for information in the past, but neither compared with what they knew down at Sissy's. It was like walking into an office of trained detectives sometimes—maybe even better. He wondered how they did it.

On his last visit, talk had turned to him and Diane. Joe was a bit surprised, as he thought they were being very discreet. He told them they were just friends, and luckily, before he had to continue the conversation too much longer, it turned to another subject—Charles Paulson and Janie Johnson. Apparently, one of the women lived near someone who lived near Janie, who saw Charles Paulson coming out of her house one evening.

"She's finally got her wish," one woman said.

"She's been after that poor man since before his wife died," another woman said.

Sissy shushed her. She didn't like it when someone brought up too negative of talk, especially when there were deaths involved—especially a murder and a suicide.

"Well, at least both people who lost a spouse don't have to be completely alone," said a woman whose husband had died two years before. "Not everyone is so fortunate," she shared sadly.

The others agreed and the subject was dropped—sort of— to talk about the upcoming church picnic at St. John's.

"I'm surprised they are even having it this year, but I suppose it's time to try to get back to some type of normal," one person said.

"Pastor Kate is doing a good job of helping the congregation," Sissy said, even though she belonged to a different congregation. "I hear she is very nice, does a lot of visiting, and is a good preacher."

Joe found himself nodding as she said that. "Don't move your head!" Sissy barked at him.

The talk then turned to the bouncy house the church planned to have this year. "Maybe that will bring back some of the families who have left."

"Hopefully. I don't like to see any churches struggling," Sissy said. "They really are pillars of our community." She spoke seriously, and everyone agreed.

When Joe had left that day, he had decided he and Diane were going to have to be even more careful when doing things together. That was how they had ended up on the bike ride around Lake Monona in Madison the prior Sunday afternoon, riding rental e-bikes. He had to admit, they were pretty neat, and since he hadn't ridden in a long time and there were a few good hills on the route, he was happy they had them that day.

Now he was wondering how he should approach the church picnic. Maybe he shouldn't even attend, if people were beginning to talk about him and Diane. He would see what transpired as the day drew closer. Maybe he'd get called in to work, and wouldn't have to worry about it at all.

***

Joe didn't have to work on Sunday, so he went to

church. He had forgotten to bring a chair or food, so he stood at the back of the group sitting on lawn chairs or blankets, which were spread out on a section of the parking lot nearest the church portico. An electronic keyboard was set up at the front, right under the portico in case there was a summer cloudburst, along with a make-shift pulpit and microphones for the preacher and musician.

It was a shorter-than-normal service. A prayer for the meal ended the service, and everyone suddenly produced a box, bag, or basket of food and walked the items over to two long tables waiting in the shade of two huge trees. A large container of lemonade and the biggest coffee pot Joe had ever seen sat at the end of one table. It didn't matter that it was eighty-some degrees and humid—coffee was a must with this bunch.

"Main dishes on this table!" a woman shouted. "Put the salads and desserts next to beverages." She was the head of the women's group, he learned, and definitely had a take-charge way about her.

The bouncy house was off to the side on a patch of grass. As the congregation had hoped, it was a big draw, and families who hadn't been in church in months had come. The children could hardly wait to get in it, but someone wisely blocked off the entrance until after they ate. The children rushed to the tables to get food, anxious to play after eating. The parents slowed them down, however, and joined them to help with their plates.

Joe was just going to leave when he saw Charles Paulson. He thought about the things he had recently learned. Charles and Janie had some sort of relationship, supposedly—and there had been some sort of land deal he wouldn't make with Simon in the past. Then he thought about Diane—her living out "near the Paulsons." Joe had taken a drive out near the Paulson farm. There were several gravel roads nearby, two with fire numbers, but he had no idea which one may have been Diane's property. He had never been to her country home, nor she to his house. He hoped one day both of those things would happen, but he wanted Diane to make the first move, so he wasn't about to bring it up.

Janie was at the picnic, too, but she and Charles had not sat with one another. Joe didn't blame them, with the way gossip moved around town. Maybe they were just in the friend stage, too, like he was with Diane.

Joe scanned the assembly for Diane. She was near the table with the beverages, in a deep discussion with the leader of the women's group, so Joe decided to go home. He hadn't brought anything to share and would feel guilty if he took part in the meal. He would call Diane later, he decided, and went home for lunch and then a run.

Later that afternoon, just as he picked up the phone to call Diane, Joe's cell phone rang. It was Oscar, the custodian at the church, on the other end of the line. He almost hadn't answered it as he didn't recognize the number, but something told him to take the call. He wondered how Oscar got his number, but then remembered he had given all the choir members whom he had interviewed his number in case they thought of something they had forgotten to tell him when they had met.

Oscar was often upset about something, but now he was beside himself. He was shouting into the phone, "You've got to come over to the church—NOW!"

Joe tried to get him to settle down, but Oscar wouldn't

listen to him. He reluctantly agreed to come over. His call to Diane would have to wait.

He pulled on a clean shirt, wishing he could shower, but he didn't think he should waste any time, as Oscar had sounded so distressed. He would be really mad if he got there and Oscar was just grumping over something silly that only Oscar thought was a big deal.

But that wasn't the case. Joe parked near the back door, where Oscar was waiting for him. Oscar didn't even say anything, just led him down the hall toward the offices. The rooms had been ransacked. Papers, pens, and pencils littered the floor. Chairs were tipped over. A drip coffee machine and ceramic mugs were smashed on the floor. Pictures lay broken, off the walls. Oscar had returned to clean up after the picnic and found the doors unlocked to the offices and the carnage inside them.

For as many people as there were who knew the key code to the back door, there were only a handful of people with access to physical keys to the offices. The current key holders included the pastor, the temporary secretary, and Oscar to both offices, and the leader of the women's group, Edward Knight, and Edner, whose job it was to lock up the offering in the secretary's office, with keys to the secretary's office only.

Joe called the unit on duty and Officer Jodie Allen arrived. She was new and was proving to be a great addition to the department. She had a bachelor's degree in Criminal Justice from UW-Platteville, was smart, had five years of work experience, and—as many of Joe's fellow male colleagues had noticed and mentioned more often than not—was quite attractive. Joe agreed, but he was not the least bit interested. His heart belonged to Diane, whether he wanted it to or not.

Jodie took down all the information from Oscar. "Is there anyone else who could possibly have a key to the office?"

Oscar thought a moment. "Not anymore. Everyone else who used to have one is either dead or left the congregation. I have no idea if they turned in their keys or not."

That made Joe think of Evelyn, sneaking in to the church via the back door months before. Or how about that former secretary—Margaret Miller? She had been very upset when she left—but why do something like this, and why now?

Jodie took down the information, took photos, then told Oscar to leave the office until further notice. She got the number of the pastor and called her, and then the secretary, and they were on their way to the church immediately.

Since the officer had everything under control, and he was technically off duty, Joe went home to shower and make his call to Diane.

As he stood in the stream of warm water, he thought about who might do something like this and why. Heck, it could have been Oscar himself. The man was very unusual, and always unhappy about something at the church. Or it could be the somewhat eccentric Evelyn Russo, who had previously gone into the church after hours, or the former secretary—both had abruptly quit their jobs and left the church after the death of the pastor. Maybe there was more to the story than just his death.

Joe was pretty sure it wasn't Edner—that man was so dedicated and honorable. But whenever he thought of

Edner these days, it brought to mind Jared. Something was still not right there—Joe just knew it in his bones. Did Jared have access to Edner's keys to the office, where the offering was stored? He hadn't asked if anything was amiss with the weekly collection, but would text Jodie to make sure she checked it out with the pastor and secretary.

After Joe finished showering and texting Jodie, he finally called Diane. She didn't answer. He was not happy at all, but then his cell rang and her name and number flashed at him.

"Hi there," she said.

"Hi, yourself," he responded.

"We missed you today. Did you have to work?"

"No. I was there for the service—standing way in the back. Forgot all about bringing a chair or food, so I left before the picnic began," he explained.

"You should have stayed. The food was wonderful, as usual. Everyone pulls out all the stoppers and there's always more than enough."

"Maybe next year," he said, hoping that next year he and Diane might be more than friends—and also able to let others know it. "I was back at the church this afternoon, though. I actually wondered if you wanted to get together, so I could talk to you more about it. It's not really a phone subject."

This piqued Diane's interest, so she suggested he come over to her house. Addie had signed up to help at the Bible Camp for grandparents/grandchildren camp. She really had no desire to spend any more time at her house than she had to before heading to college the following weekend.

Diane said she was going to have a sandwich, as she

was still full from the picnic, but she did have some casserole and pie left over from the picnic, if he wanted to try them. Joe wasn't going to turn down that offer, so he hung up the phone and hopped into his car. It was only about ten minutes to Diane's house, which was on the other side of town. Another good thing about a small town—minimal travel time.

He decided that the church discussion could wait until after the delicious casserole and strawberry rhubarb pie. Diane had made two pies to take this year, in case fewer people attended and brought food. She had hoped there would be some left, as it was her favorite. Many people had brought double batches of food items, for the same reason as Diane, so there were actually leftovers this time.

Joe even indulged in a scoop of ice cream on top of the delicious pie with the flakiest crust he'd ever had, but only one scoop. He looked and felt great, and wanted to stay that way. He thought the pie was even better than his grandma's, and that was really saying something.

Diane was perfect, he thought to himself.

After finishing the meal and discussing the relative success of the picnic and the hit of the bouncy house, Joe helped Diane clear and rinse the plates.

"You don't have to do that," she said.

"I know, but I wanted to help in some way. It's the least I could do after this great meal," he said sincerely.

"You're easy to please," she said. They dried their hands on an old, embroidered dish towel, then Diane turned to him.

"You said there was something you wanted to talk about?"

Joe wished he didn't have to bring up anything

negative about the church, but he wanted Diane to hear it first before it was all over town. He knew from his time at Sissy's that there were more people than he thought listening to the police scanner, so it was probably spreading quickly already. Maybe Diane even knew about it already.

Joe filled her in on Oscar's call and the mess at the church, then his questions about who might have done it. He said that the whole thing made him wonder if there hadn't been more of a story behind Millicent Paulson's death, even. It seemed like more people didn't like the Paulsons than he thought, or others may have wanted Millie out of their way for some reason. He thought of Janie, particularly, as he said this.

As he discussed the situation and his thoughts, Diane's countenance fell and she turned pale.

"I'm sorry," Joe said. "I'm upsetting you."

"Will this ever end?" Diane spoke so sadly it broke his heart, and her eyes began to tear up.

He wasn't sure if he should or not, but Joe found himself reaching for Diane and pulling her close to his chest for a hug. He could smell her shampoo again, one of his favorite smells on earth. His head was next to hers and his heart was beating so hard he was certain she could feel it. His hand stroked her back to comfort her when she pulled back slightly. He was sure he had made a mistake and gone too far, but instead Diane surprised Joe greatly by pulling his lips to hers for a kiss.

He was speechless afterward, and even more so when she kissed him a second time—longer and stronger.

Then Diane suddenly pulled back. "I'm sorry, Joe," she said apologetically. "I shouldn't have done that. It's too soon..."

As much as Joe wanted to go on kissing Diane for the rest of the evening and into the night, he nodded his head that he understood, even though every fiber of his body was aching for more.

"I should probably go," Joe said.

"Yes, you probably should. I don't really trust myself right now," Diane mentioned.

He hugged her gently, then let go. "I'll see you later," he said.

"You can count on it," she said.

Joe reluctantly left and Diane watched him drive away. Then she made a phone call.

"I don't know how much longer I can go on like this," she spoke into the phone.

PART III

One year earlier

(Four months before the murder)

It was the day of the annual church picnic. Even though Millie loved the winter holiday season best of all, she did enjoy this event and time of year tremendously. It was the last hurrah of the summer church season. Soon the children would be back to school, and Sunday school would be in full swing. The one mid-morning service of the summer would revert to two services, with Sunday school and a fellowship time between services.

Millie would work with the teachers on a song for the first day of class, a day referred to as "Rally Day." Then the students would sing it with her accompanying them at the late service.

Millie would be happy to see more of the young ones back at church again. She loved the little ones, and vice-versa, and felt almost motherly toward them. She had worked with many of them at Vacation Bible School, leading the music, but that had been back at the end of June. Since then, many families were absent. They used the summer months to travel, or go to family cabins for the weekend. And then, of course, there were the baseball and softball tournaments out of town that were held over the entire weekend.

Charles came into the kitchen where Millie was putting together two baskets—one with a variety of fruit tarts, the other with fried chicken and homemade buttermilk and cheesy biscuits. She loved to cook, and the large old-fashioned wicker picnic baskets would be filled to the brim with her tasty offerings.

"Millicent, you don't have to feed the entire congregation," Charles said cooly.

"You know me, I love to cook," she said, smiling. "And the people truly appreciate it."

"Oh yes, I know you. You spend more time working on projects for the church than you do on anything else."

"I am employed by the church, Charles," she said defensively.

To that, he sneered. Charles saw Millicent's work at the church as nothing more than a hobby—and one she spent way too much time on.

In his mind, Charles thought that if Millicent had concentrated more on them as a couple instead of the church, maybe they would be parents—even though he knew better.

"Maybe if you spent more time on us..." Charles didn't finish his sentence.

"Maybe I would if you were home more," Millicent retorted, feeling slighted.

"Someone's got to make some real money around here."

Millicent was tired of this argument. It wasn't the first time Charles had brought this up. He often mentioned that she should just volunteer at the church, because if one added up her compensation and divided it by all the hours she put in, she might as well have. But Millicent loved her work and the church, and especially the choir. True, it wasn't anything like the magnificent choir she had directed back in Illinois, but the people tried hard and seemed open to trying whatever she suggested. Well, maybe not Edward, but even so, he was still in the choir. She knew he didn't like the modern songs she sometimes picked out, and knew that if he was ever going to be "ill" on a Sunday, it happened to be when they were singing a praise song.

She liked the church dinners, the little food pantry that had opened a year ago that was open the last Thursday of every month or for personal emergencies, and especially the Sunday school and Vacation Bible School, also known as "VBS."

People even invited their grandchildren and neighbors to VBS, as it was well attended, well-organized, and a lot of fun for all. Millie knew, however, that the organizers began planning for the next June's session in September. There was a reason it was such a success. It was tons of work for the coordinators. Every year, just before the classes began, she would hear them complaining and saying this was going to be their "last year" doing this. But after the leaders saw the joy and the learning happening over the four nights, they always changed their minds and were ready to get back at it after a couple of months. Their endless time and effort paid off every time.

Millicent sighed and looked at the clock. Even though it was a few minutes before they actually needed to leave, she said, "It's time to go."

Charles was thinking the same thing in his mind.

***

Pastor Michael was looking forward to the church picnic. Everyone always loved this event and attended in such positive moods. The service was outdoors—unless it was pouring. It was a relaxed atmosphere, with many families attending and children milling about, even during the worship. Little ones would dance to the music, especially when the guitar played with the keyboard and Millie sang. Millie Paulson had brought such life to the congregation with her musical talents, and he thanked God for her often. She was a very special woman, indeed.

That's why he was particularly disturbed when, after the service, he saw her husband say something to her that must have been very hurtful. She stood there for a minute or two, trying to compose herself, but then he noticed her wiping away a tear, then disappear into the church. Most people were still eating, the young ones trying to rush them along as they were chomping at the bit for games.

Diane was leading the children's activities today, as she had for the past fourteen years, ever since Addie was a four-year-old. Now, Addie was off to college the next week at his and Diane's alma mater. While he was excited for his daughter, it felt like a huge personal loss. He and Addie always had a close relationship. She was kind, fun-loving, and liked the same things he did, like music, reading, writing, and soccer. She also loved the Lord, and he thought she might follow in his footsteps into the ministry one day. He would love it if she did, but hesitated to say anything about it. He would let the Holy Spirit take care of nudging her—as had been the case in his calling.

When he had gone to college, his dream had been to become a high school English teacher and soccer coach. He always loved reading and writing, and wanted to teach them to others. And soccer was his other passion. But then came one of the school's required courses on the Bible during his second semester, taught by a very special professor who made it all make sense to him for the first time. When the course was over, and after conversations with more than one person who said the same thing to him about his God-given gifts, he knew what he was called to do in life—become a pastor. From then on, he took courses that would be beneficial in seminary, and later in ministry, and worked as one of the chapel assistants at the college in between his studies and playing soccer.

Michael met Diane in choir at the beginning of his senior year. There was a song in which the choir sections were dispersed among one another. Diane landed next to him. She dropped her folder of music and he picked it up, and that was it for him. He had never believed in love at first sight before that day, but had shared their story many times over the years, especially when doing counseling with couples before their marriage. He then told them that those feelings of love were a great start, but not enough to sustain a long-term relationship. He always told them to be prepared to work on their relationship "until death do us part."

He had always been happy to have taken his own advice, but in the last year, he had started falling away from good practices, as had Diane. Something had changed. It all started at the beginning of Addie's senior year of high school.

At first, he thought Diane was experiencing "empty nest" syndrome, even before Addie left the house, but it seemed different from what others had shared with him about their children growing up and leaving home. In fact, Diane seemed to relish the idea of Addie moving on, and seemed to be pushing for their lives to change right along with their daughter's. It had gotten even worse since

Addie's graduation and her time away working at Bible Camp for the summer.

Diane had mentioned a few times throughout the year that perhaps it was time for him to take a new call. He was surprised—no, shocked—since St. John's was her home congregation of many years.

After Addie left for camp, the "new call" idea started morphing into something else—like maybe they should move away from Farmerton and both do something new. That shocked him even more, as he knew one of the attractions for Diane in their relationship had been the thought of being a pastor's spouse. Diane loved the idea right from the beginning, and until this past year, had seemed to relish the role—at least most of the time.

Michael didn't really recognize his wife anymore—the person she was becoming—and they had become more distant as the summer wore on. On several occasions he found her sleeping on the couch. She had told him he was snoring, but that had never been an issue for him. Feeling that Diane was grasping at straws, Michael had then suggested attending a Christian marriage retreat being held at a beautiful lake resort. Diane suggested he see a therapist if he was experiencing an issue, but she felt no need or desire for couples therapy, as she put it.

And this very morning on their way to church, Diane had informed him that this was the very last time she would be leading games at the church picnic, whether they were still at St. John's or not the next year.

All these things were on his mind until he saw Charles say whatever he said to Millicent, which sent her into the church. Which sent him into the church.

Michael looked down the hallways, but figured that

Millie had most likely gone to the choir room. On this way, he passed the secretary's office, and out of the corner of his eye, saw Millie standing in the corner of the room, crying.

He knocked gently on the door, then entered.

"Millie—is everything—are you—all right?" Michael asked quietly.

She shook her head.

"Would you like to talk about it?"

Again, she indicated "no" but he could sense that she wasn't being honest. So, instead of moving away from her, or leaving the room completely, Michael did everything he knew he shouldn't do. He went up to Millie and hugged her in a room with a closed door, with no one else around. It violated everything he had ever been taught in ethics class in seminary, or in subsequent training sessions in his denomination. Maybe because Millie was a member of the church staff, rather than just a parishioner, he found some way to justify it, but he knew deep down that there was absolutely no good excuse.

Millie smelled like sunshine and flowers. He held her tightly, but then gained his senses and pulled back.

"I'm sorry for whatever is making you sad, Millie. You don't deserve it. Let me know if there is anything I can do to help," he said, stepping back from her, knowing that he had been inappropriate.

"I will," she said. "Thank you. Very much." She seemed to be pulling herself together, and looked right into his eyes.

Michael took another step backward, as he felt like Millie was looking right into his soul with those beautiful eyes of hers. He wondered how anyone could treat someone like her as badly as Charles had. Millie didn't appear to have a mean bone in her body.

"Whenever you need to talk, Millie, I'm here for you," he said, then left the office, wishing he had used different words, thinking they had taken on a too-personal tone.

Michael emerged from the church doors, looking around a bit sheepishly, like a child who had just done something wrong and was waiting to see if his parents noticed. He then proceeded to join in a conversation with several other parishioners.

Then the church door opened again, and out came Millicent. She, too, looked around, then proceeded to her keyboard to retrieve her music folder.

Everyone was preoccupied, so it seemed as if no one noticed Pastor Michael or Millie. But across the parking lot, on the grass where a sack race was getting ready to begin, Diane watched her husband, then the choir director, come out of the church, both looking around with guilty looks on their faces.

***

Diane knew that Michael couldn't share details of conversations with others, but she thought that perhaps he would mention Millie at some point in the hours after the picnic, but he did not. Instead, he changed clothes and went out for a run the second he got home. While he did run from time to time, it wasn't his favorite thing to do, and certainly not on a Sunday afternoon, when he often took a nap. When he did go out for exercise, he usually preferred cycling, hiking, or swimming. He saved running for times when he felt anxious or troubled.

Michael shed his button-down collar shirt—he always wore the same kind of shirts, no matter how casual or formal the occasion, along with his khakis and loafers—and put on his running shorts and T-shirt, then hit the road. Sometimes he asked Diane to join him, but if he was trying to work something out or needed time to think, he wouldn't mention it.

Diane went up to change and was surprised when she walked into the bedroom and found Michael's church clothes on the floor. That wasn't like Michael. He was usually more tidy than she was. Diane picked them up, planning to put them on hangers, when she caught a whiff of something. It seemed somewhat familiar to her, but she just couldn't place it. She smelled both pieces of clothes. The smell was definitely coming from the shirt—the collar and shoulder area. Then she thought of Michael and Millie both coming out of the church, looking around to see if anyone noticed them. She was pretty sure, then, she knew where she had smelled that scent before. She dropped the clothes back into a pile on the floor, put the hangers away, grabbed her tennis shoes, and left the house to take a walk.

Diane tried not to jump to conclusions. It wasn't completely unlike Michael to hug a member of the church, especially his staff. He was a "hugger," even though it had become increasingly frowned upon in churches and school settings. Yet, for all the hugs he had given out, rarely did she notice a scent that strongly. If it hadn't been for the looks on their faces as they emerged from the church, she might not have even given it a second thought. She wondered if she should say something to Michael, but instead, she decided she would just watch them more closely. It was probably nothing, she thought.

Diane had to admit—Michael was a saint in that area. She had never worried about him, even though she knew that many women found him attractive. He had always seemed oblivious to other women's interest in him, whether it was in college, seminary, or the parish. Whenever Diane mentioned something that someone said or a look they had given him, he had quickly dismissed it. He always ended these conversations with "You know you're the only one for me, Diane." And he meant it.

Besides, he knew the possible consequences for inappropriate relationships could be quite serious. Michael was very dedicated to the church, and Diane thought he would rather die than be taken off the pastoral roster for misconduct. He could even lose his pension, although she knew his work in ministry and his reputation were more important to him than any monetary consequences. Still, it was a good deterrent.

Diane went home and made some tea, then sat on the porch, sitting on the old wooden swing, thinking—and praying—she was right.

***

Charles went home from the picnic and packed his new Louis Vuitton suitcase. Millicent had had a fit when he purchased it, but as he pointed out to her, they had no children to spend their money on, so he should be able to indulge in a luxury now and then. Then he reminded her of the Steinway baby grand piano sitting in their living room—his "go-to" whenever she questioned one of his expenses. If she could have one of those—never mind that it had been her anniversary gift from him on their fifth anniversary—he should be able to buy premier luggage. That had quieted her quickly, and the subject was dropped.

Charles would be in Dallas the next day for a week-long project. He couldn't wait to get on the plane out of Madison, which now had non-stop flights to the city, and wished he could will it to be the next morning. He felt like the huge "California King" he and Millicent shared was not big enough any longer. He was tired of arguing. He was tired of her sad puppy dog eyes every time he said something to her. For instance, she moped around all afternoon after they got home from the church picnic. The woman was too sensitive and too emotional. Millicent wouldn't last a day in the business world, Charles thought as he closed his suitcase.

***

A few days had passed since the picnic—and the embrace. Michael had thought of little else since. "Rally Sunday" was coming up quickly, and Millie had texted him asking if they could talk in his office. He was thankful, as he wanted to apologize for his behavior in person. There really was no other way to do it. An email could be intercepted or misinterpreted by an outside source. He knew that his secretary knew his passwords, as he had given them to her just in case of an issue. He didn't think she ever abused the privilege, but just in case, he didn't want there to be evidence of possible wrongdoing which was accessible to others. He would get this situation nipped in the bud as soon as possible.

***

Millie looked at her image in the full-length antique mirror in the bedroom, smoothing down a blouse. She had changed her clothes three times already. She didn't know why she was acting like this. She and Pastor Michael had met many times to discuss worship services, so why was she so nervous this time? Why did she care about what she would wear?

She finally decided to put on the first outfit she had worn: black slacks, white blouse, black blazer. She was working, after all, not going on a date. She put back all her other choices, grabbed her purse, and was out the door. Thank goodness Charles was out of town. He would have made a huge deal of her trying on more than one outfit. Actually, she probably wouldn't have even attempted trying on more than one if he had been in residence. He seemed to have a negative comment for everything she did these days, and she was sure this would have put him over the top.

She drove to church, thinking about Pastor Michael. He had been on her mind since the picnic. He was so kind and caring. She was certain he would never talk to his wife in the same way Charles talked to her—now on a regular basis. And then she thought about the hug.

It had felt wonderful to be touched by someone who actually cared about her. Charles had become so rude that she was having a very difficult time in the intimacy area. Not that he was very interested in the first place. It seemed like he had to have a drink or two to even get in the mood, and then she hated how aggressive he was. It didn't feel like making love anymore—and if she was honest, that went both ways. She no longer felt she loved Charles, although she still felt committed—or maybe a better word was obligated—to him. She guessed she should be thankful that Charles was gone more and more for work these days, so she didn't have to deal with any of it.

Pastor Michael was in his office when Millie arrived at church, the door to the hallway open and waiting for her arrival. She started toward one of the two chairs on the opposite side of his desk, often used by couples who were doing pre-marriage counseling. She didn't close the door behind her, as he always told her leave it open, but this time he asked her to please close it. She walked back to the door and shut it. The blinds to the hallway and the adjoining secretary's office were open, though. This was how it usually was for a normal counseling session. If there was some other type of extraordinary circumstance or confidential meeting with someone, the blinds would be closed, but that was a rarity.

"Millie, before we talk about special music, I just wanted to apologize for last Sunday," Pastor Michael said.

Before he could go on, Millie spoke. "And I just wanted to *thank* you for last Sunday. It meant a lot to me that you...cared. You asked me if everything was okay. It wasn't—and it still isn't. It hasn't been for a long time." Millie then went on to tell him about Charles, and his always arguing and usually bringing up not being able to have children. And then she mentioned that the doctor had said the chance of Charles' fathering a child would be nothing short of a miracle. She thought Charles was taking out his disappointment on her, trying to put blame where there wasn't really any, because he just couldn't come to terms with the idea that he was not perfect—at least not in his eyes.

"Charles is a perfectionist, especially when it comes to

things he finds most important. He is very hard on himself—and others," she added quietly. She told him briefly about her suggestion to adopt, but his refusal to explore that option.

Pastor Michael used his usual line when there were no good answers to someone's problems, wanting her to know that someone was listening, and that someone cared. "I'm sorry you are experiencing this, Millie." In his mind, he added, *You don't deserve this—and he doesn't deserve you.* "Whenever you need to talk, please let me know." Millie nodded that she would.

They moved on to the music for Rally Day. Choir practice began the next evening, which would give them two rehearsals before they sang the piece in church. The Sunday school children would learn a song that morning and sing it at the second service. This one would have hand motions with it, which Millie thought the kids would love. Pastor Michael watched her and how excited and animated she got when she spoke about the children singing, and thought how unfair it was that she wasn't a mother, and that she probably never would be.

They were done with business talk, and both needed to get on with their work for the afternoon. Millie planned to meet with Evelyn after her school day ended to go over the music, as Evelyn would accompany both the choir and the children. Pastor Michael planned to do his text study for Sunday's sermon.

Millie sat forward in her chair, getting ready to stand up. Then she instinctively put her hand on top of Pastor Michael's. "Thank you, again—so much," she said, then suddenly noticed what she had done and removed her hand. "I'll see you tomorrow evening at choir rehearsal," she said, rising from her chair.

It took Pastor Michael a moment to gather his wits about him. "Um, yes. See you tomorrow evening." He stood and watched Millie leave. He looked to see if his secretary, Margaret Miller, had been watching, but her back was to him and she was engrossed in working on the Sunday bulletin on her computer. The volunteer "bulletin folders," two older widows, would be in the next morning to get them ready for Sunday.

He sat back down, still feeling Millie's hand on top of his. After ten minutes of just sitting at his desk, his phone alerted him to his text study. Usually, he did his study on his own, but once a month he got together with other pastors in the area to discuss Sunday's readings, or what they were doing for a special season. They also caught up on one another's families and supported each other, if there was a problem someone was facing in the parish or at home. He usually looked forward to this time and couldn't wait to get together, but today he found himself texting the leader for that month, saying something had come up and he wouldn't be joining them.

It wasn't a complete lie. Something—*someone*—had come up. Her name was Millicent Paulson.

***

Charles had had a lot of time to think on his business trip to Dallas. After a few days of successful meetings, delicious dinners at top-notch restaurants, and a couple of rounds of golf, he was in a much better mood. He pondered why he was always so angry with—and nasty toward—Millicent. He always had great intentions to be civil when he went home. Sometimes he even came back with a gift for Millicent, his version of saying he was sorry—words he just couldn't seem to get past his lips. He felt bad about how he felt and acted at home, but the moment he returned home, the feelings returned right with him. They were an unfortunate combination of disappointment and hostility.

If Charles had been able to predict the future when they had returned to Wisconsin, he never would have left the Chicago area. Both he and Millicent had enjoyed their time in Naperville very much. Everything about it was wonderful—their house, neighborhood, golf courses, restaurants, and their church. Millicent's position as choir director demanded a lot of time, but at least she had very competent musicians to work with, and the end product was always outstanding.

If Charles had known it wouldn't make any difference in the child-bearing department, he never would have suggested they move back to his hometown and wouldn't have made the changes he made at work, either. He had purposely transitioned into a branch of his company that was more family-friendly, with fewer and usually shorter trips to often less-attractive destinations. He had wanted to be home more often for the family he thought Millicent and he would have by this time, which had never materialized.

So whenever he came back to their current reality, his negative feelings and behaviors came back, too—often with little provocation. And it had been getting worse over the past few months. Unfortunately, rather than working on a solution, he began to avoid his wife and home, asking for more assignments out of town and taking on projects no one else cared to do. He was almost making as much as he was in his previous position, but even so, there was little joy in the money anymore. Something was lacking in his life, but he just didn't know what it was—not yet, anyway.

***

Diane couldn't shake the smell on Michael's shirt from her mind, especially when Wednesday night's choir rehearsal came around. It was their first one back after their summer hiatus, so everyone was excited. Millie handed out music folders to everyone and showed off a new wooden holder for the folders which the "Morning Men" had built. The group of mostly retired gentlemen met every Tuesday morning for breakfast, a devotion, and occasionally decided on a project to work on in the church or community.

The music holder was their newest accomplishment, and one of which they were quite proud. It not only looked nice, but it definitely beat stacking the folders on a countertop, with everyone waiting to paw through them. Now everyone had a numbered folder, which would be deposited into a slot with the corresponding number at the end of each rehearsal, and easily retrieved. The choir members were very pleased with the gift.

Normally, Diane would have volunteered to write a thank you note to the men's group from the choir. She knew for a fact, as Michael often joined them, that they appreciated and read each and every such note at their meetings. But today, she passed on the idea. She was tired of always being the one to think of such things and carry them out. It was someone else's turn.

Plus, she was more interested in watching any interactions between her husband and Millie.

She watched Millie carefully as she handed out the folders to each member, smiling and speaking directly to each member of the choir as she did so—to everyone except Michael. She seemed to hand off the folder as quickly as possible, careful not to make eye contact. Maybe it was just her imagination, Diane thought at first. But during the entire rehearsal, Millie never looked Michael's way. Diane decided she would watch again the next week. Maybe this was just a coincidence.

Michael was quiet on the way home from church, which was only a few blocks away from the parsonage. Usually, he was effusive about the music and other planned activities for Rally Sunday, but he seemed preoccupied. Perhaps he and Millie had had a disagreement over something—maybe whatever happened the past Sunday—or about plans for the start of the choir and Sunday school season. Diane decided to stay out of it, whatever *it* was.

They arrived home and Michael went straight to his study. Diane went to read her book in the living room. She was almost finished and would be sorry when she was done with this one. It was an engrossing murder mystery, her "guilty pleasure," as she referred to the reading of this genre. A librarian had put her on to her first such book, and she had been hooked ever since.

An hour passed and Diane finished the book and set it down on the table next to the chair with a sigh and a smile. She again had solved the murder before the ending—she was really good at that sort of thing. Diane had been so engrossed in the story that she hadn't even noticed Michael had yet to come out of the study. Usually, he was done with devotions and prayers within a half-hour to forty-five minutes, but not on this night.

She knocked gently on the door, wanting to make sure he was okay. She worried he was sick. It would be really bad timing if he was ill, as they would be taking Addie to college in just a couple of days.

Addie was currently out with her high school friends. They had been getting together every evening this week, enjoying each other's company and sending each other off, one by one.

Addie was one of the last in her friend group to leave for school, so she had been orchestrating the goodbye gatherings. The previous night they had gathered at their family cabin in the country doing a cookout and campfire, with Diane and Michael supervising. Tonight they were at Addie's best friend's house.

The door to the study opened slowly and Michael looked at her. She hadn't seen that look on his face in a long time. Michael pulled her into the study, shut the door, and kissed her passionately, backing her against the door and pressing hard against her. Just then they heard Addie come into the house.

Addie called out to them. "Anybody home?"

Michael backed away from Diane, and they both pulled themselves together, feeling like teenagers caught by their parents, rather than the other way around.

"We're in here," Diane called, and Michael quickly sat down at his desk and computer as Diane started opening the door.

"You're home early," Diane said to Addie.

"Molly is leaving tomorrow, so her mom said we had to leave so Molly could finish packing."

"Speaking of packing up, how is *your* packing going?" Diane asked her daughter, giving her a little hug.

"I knew you were going to ask that. It's *going*. I'll do some more tonight and finish it tomorrow—I promise. But, first—ice cream! Anyone else with me?" she asked before she started for the kitchen.

"Sure," said Diane.

"I'll be there in a minute," Michael called from his desk. "You know I can't pass that up."

It was one of their favorite family traditions over the years, and in two days, Addie would be off to college. So, the three enjoyed ice cream in the kitchen, not knowing it was the very last time they would ever do that together.

***

Diane and Michael had gotten Addie off to school, enjoying walking around the very campus where they met, dated, and fell in love. They took many photos of their daughter and of the three of them together in favorite spots for photos. They took her for an ice cream cone at a shop that had opened when they were in college, which they had frequented often in their year together at school. They even sat at "their table."

Michael had not been a "drinker," even though he legally could have been at age twenty-one. It's not that he didn't like alcohol, but he couldn't handle it well—especially not his favorite—Irish whiskey. He couldn't seem to stop drinking it, and would sometimes imbibe until he passed out. He sometimes still had a bit of whiskey in his coffee on a cold winter's day, or for a celebration, but only when Diane was around to cut him off. Thus, he had decided back in college that ice cream would be his guilty pleasure, and had stuck with it over the years.

The trip to drop off Addie had been an almost perfect day. The sun was shining and the air was warm and pleasant. A few of the maples' leaves were just beginning to turn, signaling the dawn of autumn. To say that Addie was excited would be an understatement. She chatted away with the students who were helping the first-years move in. The move-in was incredibly quick due to volunteers carrying all of Addie's belongings to her room for her. Diane had imagined sore backs after this day, but she and Michael hardly touched a box. That had given them the time for their "nostalgia tour" and ice cream. Afterward, they left Addie and her roommate to unpack, decorate, and get to know each other.

It had been a wonderful day, but the ride home had been a departure from the tone of the early part of the day. Michael was silent on the almost two-hour trip home from Iowa. Diane thought he might be upset about leaving Addie, so she didn't push it.

But then the rest of the week happened, and Michael was still subdued. He barely said a word—and had barely touched her—since that evening in his study. That was why she had decided to watch him closely that evening at choir rehearsal—to look for any clues to what was making him clam up. She wondered if perhaps he was contemplating her suggestions of taking a new call—or doing something else completely unrelated to parish ministry. Maybe he was feeling guilty about those ideas. Perhaps he had confided in Millie, which could explain the recent behavior. Or then her mind flitted back to earlier thoughts—maybe something had happened before Michael and Millie had exited the church the day of the picnic.

Diane wasn't naive. She was highly aware that women found her husband attractive, especially in the past few years. He was one of those late bloomers, who seemed to get more handsome and rugged-looking in his forties than he ever did in his twenties or thirties. She knew that his secretary, Margaret, was infatuated with him, treating him like royalty and watching him whenever she thought no one else was looking.

And Millicent—she was gorgeous—that was without question. Men had a difficult time keeping their eyes off her. An attraction to her would be completely understandable.

So, Diane watched Michael—and Millie and Michael—at rehearsal, but everything seemed back to normal this time. There were no more averted looks or sheepish glances. Perhaps she had been imagining things the previous week.

When they got home, Diane sat down in the reading chair once again to begin her new murder mystery, and Michael went to his study. He used to sit near her and read a book, too, or talk, but they hadn't shared words all week. She and Michael used to be able to talk so freely, and she had often thought of him as an "open book." Now, it was like that book had been slammed completely shut.

Diane vacillated between being upset with him, to not caring at all. She was starting to look into her own ideas and concentrate on her own future desires, including the possibility of beginning her own CPA firm, or possibly going back to school and getting a degree in a completely different area. She had married Michael at such a young age, then had a baby within a year. Ever since, she had put Michael, Addie, and the church first. Now, Diane felt, it was her turn.

***

It was two weeks later, and Millie couldn't stop thinking about Michael—that's how she thought of him these days, rather than Pastor Michael. She had taken to stopping into his office almost every day, closing the door behind her so they could talk without being overheard. She shared more and more of her life at home with Charles, their inability to have a family, and Charles' growing resentment and negative behavior toward her.

She always felt so much better after she shared what was on her heart with him. Michael was such a good listener and exhibited much empathy, and she needed someone to listen to her and to care. Her husband certainly did not.

Each time she and Michael met, she not only felt better, but felt something she hadn't felt in a very long time—appreciated and loved. Millie knew she shouldn't, but each time before she left his office, she touched him. Sometimes it was just her hand landing lightly on his, or on his arm or shoulder. Whenever they had a conversation, she found herself sitting or standing just a little bit closer to him. She craved physical touch, which was now non-existent at home. She hadn't realized what a void this had been in her life until she felt the warmth of his body, even if it was only in small and rather innocent ways.

She was so grateful to Michael. Not only did he make

Millie feel cared for, but respected. Michael complimented her on her work, which was the opposite of Charles' reaction whenever the subject arose. While he still participated in choir, he constantly criticized the group and thought of her work at the church as a joke, rather than a legitimate job, and certainly didn't buy into the idea of it qualifying as "music ministry."

Michael, on the other hand, always seemed to understand that the music was amazingly good for such a small congregation. He knew many others of similar size who had no choir or even a few talented musicians. She felt validated when she was at church, not only by him, but by the congregation as a whole, who seemed to appreciate the music ministry at St. John's. If it wasn't for the pastor, choir, and other church members, she wasn't sure if she could stay in Farmerton—thoughts that had never crossed her mind until the past year.

She had been dedicated to Charles, but also very reliant on him, since her parents died many years ago. Lately, she felt like he was taking advantage of this dedication, and she wasn't sure how much longer she could keep up what was feeling more and more like a charade at home.

At least there was choir practice to look forward to that evening. She put a new song into each of the music folders, left the choir room, and headed home.

Once she got to the farmhouse, Charles was in their bedroom packing a bag again, this time just a carry-on.

"Getting ready for your trip tomorrow?" Millie asked.

"No. I am preparing for my trip right this evening," Charles responded.

"This evening? But you'll miss choir rehearsal."

Charles sneered. "Millicent, the song we are singing on Sunday is for beginners. I practiced it last week. That should be sufficient. I'll be back by Friday afternoon. I was able to secure an earlier flight, so I am taking advantage of the opportunity." He closed the case, picked it up along with his briefcase, and started for the stairs.

Millicent was surprised, but not surprised at the same time. Charles hadn't even said goodbye. She tried not to feel hurt, but she couldn't help but feel slighted.

She went to the kitchen and made herself a cup of coffee. If she hadn't had rehearsal, it would have been a glass of wine. She sat in a chair overlooking the backyard, which was getting more colorful day by day. The spot by the window was her refuge, and it often made her feel better. However, today, even the scenery could not improve her mood. She couldn't wait to get to choir practice, where she would be around people who appreciated her. And she would be around Michael.

***

Michael went home early. He would do his own text study in his home office.

"Michael, Addie wants me to bring her formal dress and shoes for an event they are having on campus Friday night, so I'm off to Iowa," Diane announced as he walked in the door.

"Does it have to be now? It's choir rehearsal night."

"I know, I'm sorry. I texted Millie that I would be absent. I have a dental appointment tomorrow in the late morning, and a Sunday school meeting tomorrow evening, so it's now or never. I'm meeting Addie for pizza at

Toby's," she added, carrying the long dress bag draped over her arm, a bag with the shoes that went with it, and her purse slung over her shoulder.

Michael opened the door between the kitchen and the garage for his wife. In the past, they had always kissed goodbye, or at least hugged, but they hadn't touched each other in almost a month now, and he felt no desire to at this moment, either.

He shut the door and heard the garage door go up, and then back down. Michael walked to his study and sat down at his large, mahogany roll-top desk. He picked up his large study Bible and a few books on Matthew and made a pile next to a notepad. He knew he should get to the texts, but Michael was deep in thought. He couldn't wait to get to choir practice. He loved the music. He loved the people. And he especially—as he had come to realize earlier that day—loved the choir director.

***

Millie believed the choir sounded better than ever that evening, despite having two members, Diane and Charles, absent. Then again, the thought had crossed her mind that it sounded better *because* her husband was not in attendance. Charles' voice, even though it was pleasant to many an ear, had begun to sound like nails on a chalkboard to her.

They sang through their piece for Sunday several times at the beginning of the hour, then worked on individual sections. The basses always had the toughest time, so their part alone took about ten minutes, and the others were starting to get antsy and chatty. Millie changed then to sight-reading another song for their next performance, then came back to Sunday's piece two more times before they called it a night. Afterward, the members put their folders away in the new holder and began walking out to their cars in the back lot. Evelyn Russo dawdled, trying to spend a bit of extra time with Millie, but finally put her music in her case and went home. She knew she had recently overstepped her boundaries with Millie, and their relationship had been strained ever since.

Millie waited for Evelyn to leave and watched out the window as her car pulled out of the back parking lot. Evelyn was the last of the choir members to leave, except for Pastor Michael, whose car was still in the lot. He had stopped in his office to look for something in his files.

Millie finally took her music bag and purse and left the choir room. As she started walking past the offices, Michael came out of his office with a file folder in his hand, and they literally ran into one another.

"I'm so sorry," they exclaimed simultaneously, both bending down to pick up the papers from Michael's folder, which had spewed across the floor. As Millie bent down, some of the contents from the top of her purse spilled as well, and they started to laugh as they gathered up the spillages.

They stood up and looked at each other. "We're quite the pair," Millie said, handing him some papers as he handed her a hairbrush.

"We certainly are," he agreed. As he said this, his hand touched hers and it was like a bolt of lightning had hit him. His smile faded and a serious look crossed his face, then Millie's.

"Millie," he said softly.

She turned and put her belongings on the small table used for counting the offering, then took the folder from his hands and did the same, then turned around and moved closer to him. She put her fingers lightly on his cheek, and his hand came up to hers. At first, she thought he was going to move her hand away, but instead, he held it tightly and pulled her closer and kissed her. It all happened so quickly. And then it was a done deal.

She kissed him back, and then kissed him again and said goodnight. She took her purse and bag off the table and hurried to her car, afraid of what might happen if she was to stay. Michael was dumbfounded. He had not expected to do anything like this. He had never been unfaithful to Diane, at least not physically. He knew he had not been the best husband in the past year in other ways. His and Diane's relationship had really gone south, especially this summer, and the past few weeks had been the absolute low point of their marriage.

Michael didn't say a word as she left. He didn't know exactly what to say. In some ways, he wanted to say he was sorry, but he realized at that moment that deep down he wasn't sorry. Michael finally gathered himself together enough to pick up his folder, walk to his car, and start the engine. He drove home in a daze, wondering how he had gotten there when he arrived at the house.

Diane was still gone and wouldn't be home for hours. He tried to do his devotions and prayers, but couldn't concentrate. All he could think about was kissing Millie. His thoughts fluctuated between ecstasy and shame. Finally, he said his prayers for those in the congregation who needed them most, and then for himself, and went to bed, even though it was early. He wanted to be asleep when Diane got home, and even though it took him an hour to calm down and finally fall asleep, he got his wish.

***

Diane tip-toed into the bedroom just before midnight. She had had a wonderful time with Addie. They ate pizza and then stopped for ice cream. She thought she would leave out that detail when she told Michael, as he would be envious. Then they went to one of the lounges of Addie's dorm and just talked. Before they knew it, it was nine-thirty, and Addie still had some reading to do. They hugged and kissed goodbye, and Diane was on her way.

Diane stepped into the walk-in closet and shut the door behind her, turning on the light so as to not wake up her husband. She stripped off her clothes and slipped on a nightshirt. As she bent over to put her discarded clothes in the wash hamper, she caught a familiar whiff. She had smelled this smell before, several weeks before, the day of the picnic. It was Millie's perfume, she was sure of it. In some ways it would make sense, as he had been at choir practice with her.

Diane looked at Michael's shirt, which was on the top of the small pile of clothes, and put it to her nose. The shirt smelled heavily of the perfume, especially around the collar and shoulder areas. Diane put the shirt back, dropping it like it was a hot potato, and put her own clothes on top of it. She opened the closet door, turned off the light, and walked quietly to the bed.

Michael was sleeping soundly, facing her side of the bed. She gently pulled back the covers and slid in as carefully as she could. He didn't even flinch. She turned and faced him, and moved in closer to Michael, and then stopped. The smell. It was in her bed. It was on his face or his hair, or both. All she knew was she could not stay in the bed that night.

She slipped out and went to the guest room and laid down. She wondered what she should do? Should she confront Michael about this? A part of her didn't really want to know if anything was going on. She wasn't even sure how much she cared, but still—almost twenty years of marriage. She didn't have any answers. Her mind was swirling, then she got an idea. She would call Charles Paulson.

PART IV

Present Day

Joe was awake well before his alarm went off Monday morning. He had barely slept, having tossed and turned all night while thinking about Diane. Had yesterday been real? Had Diane really invited him to her home? And most of all, had she really kissed him?

Normally, he would work out before his shower, but he knew better than to lift weights when preoccupied. He didn't want to get hurt or put a dent in his floor like he had one time. So he hopped into the shower. He ate a bowl of cereal, but on the way to work, he couldn't remember what kind he had had. He thought it was a good thing there wasn't any rat poison in the same cupboard, or he might have eaten it by mistake. He was ridiculously out of it.

He checked into the office and was met by Officer Jodie. She was a breath of fresh air in the cream brick building, to say the least. She smiled at him and handed him written copies of her reports from the afternoon before. After she took photos in the church office and interviewed the pastor and acting secretary, she had gone to see the former employees who might have still had access to the offices—Evelyn Russo and Margaret Miller.

Both claimed to have been out of town that afternoon, although neither could come up with any witnesses to verify the facts. Evelyn said she was on a hike in a remote natural area, and Margaret said she had gone for a long drive during the time the event would have occurred. Joe thought it was strange that neither could come up with some type of verification of their whereabouts, so he decided he would keep an eye on both of them over the next week, and also pay special attention to the back door of the church. His mind popped back to Evelyn sneaking into the church, and wasn't completely convinced she was telling him the truth. Then again, he didn't completely trust Margaret, either, who had abruptly left the church after twenty-five years of service. It was no secret that she had been very upset when she quit.

Joe watched Jodie walk away. She was not only attractive, but best of all, she was a top-notch deputy, and was turning out to be a great asset to the department. He wasn't sure why she chose their county to live and work in, but he sure was happy that she did. He would have to ask her sometime how she ended up in the area.

Joe's thoughts were brought back to attention by a call to a fender-bender at the intersection of two county roads, so he was off and running and happy to have something else to think about for a little while. The Millie Paulson/Pastor Michael drama was finally getting to him. He had started to let go of all of it until the mishap at the church pushed it back into the light again. And he needed to get Diane out of his mind for a while, too, even though thoughts of her were pleasant—albeit *too* pleasant.

***

Two weeks had passed. Joe had seen Diane at church, but there had been no other communication between them. He just hoped and prayed the kiss hadn't ruined things for the future, although Diane had been friendly toward him when they were together at coffee hour, which was encouraging. She smiled warmly at him, so he thought they might be okay in the long run.

Joe knew that Addie was keenly on Diane's mind. It was the beginning of the school year and Addie was back at college, and happily so. As Diane put it, Addie wanted to be anywhere but Farmerton, and especially not at home. It had been a bit better for her daughter now that they were officially out of the parsonage, but still, it was hard for Addie to be around anything that reminded her too much of her father. According to Diane, Addie was now in an anger stage of grief, and Joe thought she had every right to be angry. It was a rotten situation.

Joe still wondered how it all had happened. He had been hanging out near the church building after hours, even when he wasn't on duty. He was watching that back door like a hawk, looking to see if Evelyn or Margaret or anyone tried to get in to the church after hours. No one tried to get in, but he had noticed a vehicle coming up out of the cemetery a couple of the times he drove by, but never got a very good look at it until one night while on duty.

Joe had nothing better to do, so he took an open three-to-eleven shift, grateful for the time-and-a-half pay for overtime. He had started a vacation fund at the bank, and already had a hundred dollars saved. He had a regular deposit set up into it every month and would put any extra pay into it. He wondered what type of places Diane would like to visit, then hoped he hadn't jinxed anything by getting way ahead of himself.

It was getting darker earlier, one of the drawbacks of fall, which otherwise was his favorite time of year. He parked his cruiser a block from the back exit to the church and watched. He waited for an hour, and was just about to leave when he saw a car drive up from the cemetery. One could barely make it out as it didn't have its lights on, even though it was almost completely dark. It either had been down there a long time, or had come in from the entrance down at the other side, as he hadn't seen it drive in. As it came a bit closer, he got a good look at it and found it was familiar to him. Joe recognized it as belonging to Evelyn Russo.

Joe pulled his cruiser quickly into the parking lot and cut her off. Evelyn slammed on the brakes. Joe got out of his unit and walked to her window, which she rolled down.

"Is there a problem, deputy?" Evelyn asked.

"You don't have your lights on. I didn't want you to go out on the street without them," he said, which was true.

"Okay," she said, sounding relieved, and turned them on. "Now, may I leave?"

"Yes, but do you mind if I ask you a question?"

"That's a question in itself," she said snidely.

"True. But another one?"

Evelyn stared at him, looking annoyed. "If you must."

"Have you been here recently—at night?"

She hesitated to answer. "Yes—is that a crime?"

"No, but what do you do here?"

"I'm visiting a grave, if you must know."

"Oh, sorry. Do you come here often?"

She hesitated again. Evelyn didn't want to say that she had been there almost every day for months now.

Joe could sense she was reluctant to answer, so he continued. "I just wondered if you noticed anything suspicious? Any people or vehicles near the church, or someone trying to get in the back door who shouldn't be there?"

"Does this have anything to do with the office incident I was already interrogated about?"

Joe didn't answer right away, but steered the conversation back to what Evelyn was doing there.

"You have family buried here?" Joe asked.

"No family—just a close friend. Now, I've got to get home, Sergeant. I have school tomorrow morning."

Joe had heard that Evelyn now taught in a neighboring community. They were thrilled to have her, as music teachers were hard to find, and good ones even harder.

"Goodnight, then. Remember to turn on your lights. And if you ever notice anything unusual on one of your visits, please give me a call," Joe said, producing a business card with his contact information on it.

Evelyn didn't respond, rather she turned on her lights and waited for him to get out of her way so she could head out of the driveway.

Joe pulled to the side and watched as she left. Evelyn was a stunning woman, but she was very unusual. Who was she visiting in the cemetery? he wondered. He watched her drive out of sight, then instead of going back on the road, he went down the lane into the graveyard. It wasn't his favorite place to be, especially at night. He had no idea what he expected to see, as it was now completely dark, with only a quarter-moon.

He drove past his grandparents' graves, smiling as he thought of them. He sure missed them, especially his grandma. He knew her longer and better, as his grandpa had died fifteen years before she had. He wished now he had spent more time with his grandpa. He never considered he might not be around when he was old enough to figure out what was most important in life—like family. He'd been thinking a lot about families lately. He finally felt like he was ready to settle down and have one of his own.

That made him think about Millie Paulson, and her being pregnant when she was murdered. How sad that must have been for Charles—to find out she was finally pregnant and then was gone.

As he drove by the section of the cemetery where he knew the Paulson family was buried, he decided to stop. He didn't really know why, something just told him to do it.

He got his flashlight out and headed toward the new headstone which had recently been put up with Charles and Millicent's names, birthdates, and Millie's date of death. He stopped short when his flashlight hit an object on top of the grave just under her side of the stone. He picked up a white rose and smelled its sweet scent. It was very fresh.

He then remembered Evelyn's words about visiting the grave of a close friend. He imagined Millie and Evelyn may have been very close, as they had worked together for at least five years. He put the flower back and decided he was going to keep watching. He didn't know what was going on, but he was going to get to the bottom of this, preferably sooner than later.

***

The next day Joe was due for a trim at Sissy's. On the way in, he ran into Janie Johnson, who was beaming as she hurried past him.

Joe entered the salon, where the tongues were wagging.

"If I was going to get together with someone who just lost his wife six months ago, I wouldn't be spreading it all over town," one woman remarked.

"It's not all over town—it's only here," said another.

"Same thing," said Sissy. "Joe, take a seat."

The first patron spoke again. "Then again, I guess Janie is widowed, too. But her husband died a few years ago, not less than a year ago. It just doesn't seem right to me."

"Oh, Alma, nothing ever seems quite right to you," Sissy said, and the subject was dropped as Joe sat down.

Joe couldn't help but think about the situation. So Janie was getting her dream man, after all, he thought. Or at least a shot at it. He wondered what the women in the salon would think if they knew how interested he was in Diane, who had been widowed even more recently.

"Did your department ever find out who vandalized the church office?" Sissy asked.

"Not yet," Joe answered.

"There sure has been a lot of crime around here lately. Maybe all these things are connected somehow," said another woman.

"You read too many of those mystery novels, Sylvie," answered Sissy.

"Well, you know, some of those stories aren't that far-fetched!" Sylvie added in her defense.

The subject was dropped and Joe's hair was done. Sissy was a whiz with the scissors—her salon was aptly named. Sissy took a hairdryer and blew the stray hairs off his neck and poncho and he was ready to pay and get out of there.

Joe had to admit to himself, he'd had some of the same

thoughts, but every avenue seemed to come to a dead end. Perhaps he should start reading some of those mystery books—maybe then he could solve his own unsolved and questionable cases.

***

Joe drove past the church on his way out of town. It was an office day, so there were a couple of cars parked in the back lot. Everything looked normal. He decided he would come by that evening and watch for Evelyn, or whoever else might be going to Millie's grave. Who knows—it may have been her husband who left the flower.

Joe was disappointed that evening that no one came to the grave. He decided he was going to go to the cemetery every night until he saw someone, even though it was going to be a major pain in the rear. He would park outside the cemetery's back entrance and walk in and watch.

So he did. Three nights passed, and no one came to the grave. He was tired of hiding behind bushes and the cemetery made him uncomfortable. Just when he was about to give up, on the fourth night, a car approached down the dark lane with no lights on. He checked to make sure he was concealed by the bush and watched as Evelyn Russo emerged from the vehicle. She looked around and then slowly walked to the grave, a white rose in her hand.

"I'm so sorry, Millie," she said as she bent down and placed the fresh flower on the grave in the same spot the previous one had lain, putting the old one in a plastic grocery bag she produced from her jacket pocket.

Just then a rabbit ran to the bush where Joe was hiding, startling him.

"What the hell!" Joe whispered loudly.

Evelyn jumped to her feet and faced the bushes, equally startled.

She shouted, "Who's there? I've got a weapon, so don't do anything stupid!"

Joe stepped out from the bush. "It's just me, Evelyn. Joe Zimmerman."

"Are you spying on me?" Evelyn asked angrily.

"I was watching the grave. You're the one who showed up."

"I'm not doing anything wrong, officer."

"Well, technically, you're here after dusk, and that's against the cemetery's rules, but nothing criminal. I do have a question for you, though. What are you sorry for?"

"What?"

"You said you were sorry to Millie. What are you sorry about?"

"It's none of your business, quite frankly," Evelyn retorted.

"It is if it hurt Millie."

"You think I could have *hurt* Millie? I *loved* Millie."

Just then Joe thought about what the men down at Bud's had said about Evelyn, that she preferred women over men. *Could it have been a crime of passion? If she couldn't have Millie, no one could?*

Evelyn continued, "She deserved more in this world than she received. Married to that ass, Charles. Him, always badgering her about not having a baby when he was the one who couldn't father one."

Joe's head jerked back at this news. "What do you mean?"

"They tried over and over with no results. The doctors

told them it would be one in over a million chances that they could have a baby. Something with Charles' sperm count."

Joe was quiet for a moment as he took in this information. He remembered Charles Paulson's reaction when he heard the news that Millie had been pregnant. And he remembered Pastor Michael's, as well. Joe wondered if the pregnancy was a miracle, or if Charles was not the father of the baby. If that were the case, perhaps Pastor Michael was the father. That might have been a motive for killing Millie, and later himself. All of a sudden, it seemed more and more likely that it was indeed a murder-suicide scenario as it had been deemed, and it made Joe feel angry, then very sad.

Joe thought about Diane. She would be horrified and deeply saddened if she thought Millie's baby had been her husband's. So Joe decided when he went home, he would not share what Evelyn had told him. He loved Diane and did not want to cause her such pain. He would keep it to himself. Besides, it wasn't factual—it was hearsay at this point.

"I'm sorry to have bothered you, Ms. Russo," Joe said. "Goodnight." He walked down the gravel lane toward his car in a daze.

When Joe returned home, he sat down in his old, worn La-Z-Boy and tried to watch some of the Brewers game, but couldn't seem to concentrate. He just kept thinking about the baby possibly not being Charles' own flesh and blood. The team was winning by four runs in the bottom of the eighth inning and playing out west, so after half an hour, he called it a night.

Joe crawled into his king-sized bed and stared at the

ceiling for hours. Just when he thought he might be able to fall asleep, another thought popped into his head. What if Charles had known Millie was pregnant? If so, he would have known it most likely was not his. What if he suspected the pastor and his wife were having an affair? Then he thought about Janie Johnson, beaming because she had a date with Charles. Was this something Charles had hoped for, too, before Millie's death? It seemed to Joe both those things could be motives for murder. But then again, Charles had been cleared.

Even so, Joe decided he would look over all the information on file about Charles the first thing the next morning—which was now only hours away. And that's exactly what he did.

***

For the second time, Janie came away from her date with Charles feeling disappointed. She had hoped Charles would kiss her this time, but again, he said it was too soon, and that people would talk if things progressed too quickly with them. He had come to her home for dinner again. She wore the sexiest outfit she owned and cooked a special meal.

She had been taking cooking lessons and made one of her favorite new recipes—roast beef with shallots and red wine, along with a Calcannon side dish and a fresh salad. She served sorbet for dessert, as the meal was on the heavy side.

Charles had been impressed, and had been very talkative during the meal, discussing some of his favorite restaurants he visited when he traveled for business. He had even said her meal rivaled some of them.

For the first time, he spoke of his family. He told her about his oldest nephew, who at age fourteen was already getting noticed by college cross-country coaches. He wondered out loud if he had had a son, if he would have been a good runner like his nephew, or like Charles had been in high school. When Charles said this he looked so sad, and Janie had put her hand on top of his. And he did not remove it.

For the first time, she thought she and Charles were developing something very special, so that was why she was disappointed when he wouldn't get physical with her when they said goodnight. She wanted to kiss him so badly. Actually, she wanted to do a lot more than kiss him, but now she knew she would have to continue to wait for that. But she was determined, and decided that Charles was worth the wait.

PART V

Two months before Millie's death

Pastor Michael sat in his study, staring at his devotion book. He had just forced himself to pray for the members of the congregation, something he had never experienced before. It usually was his favorite time of the day, but he couldn't help but feel guilty as he read the names on his list, wondering what the members of his flock would think about his recent behavior in thought, word, and deed.

Over the past two months, he and Millie had what he considered stolen moments. Whenever they were alone together in the building, it was a gentle touch, a hug that was longer than it should have been, a hand on a shoulder, and then the kiss after choir, when both their spouses had been absent. He felt like he had been on fire ever since, and didn't know how to stop the blaze.

Their almost daily conversations became more intimate. They shared about their lives—their past, their present, and what they hoped for in the future. Michael had hoped that these conversations would help them remember they had spouses—and in his case, a daughter— and help them come to their senses. But so far, it only seemed to draw them deeper into feelings for one another. And Michael was pretty certain at this point that he had fallen deeply in love with Millie.

He told himself it had to end, so he had called Millie and told her they needed to talk—alone, and not anywhere near the church.

Millie told him Charles was out of town and he could come to her house. He hesitated, then thought there were limited options as to where they could meet. He often visited members in their homes, so this wouldn't be seen as uncommon or strange if anyone were to find out he had been there. They were meeting the next day just after lunch. He was going to tell Millie that this had to stop—all of it. He even thought about putting in his papers for a new call, but deep down he knew he didn't want to do that. He loved the congregation. Everything was going so well. And to be truthful, Michael also didn't want Millie completely out of his life. He had convinced himself they could go back to the friendly yet professional relationship they had maintained for years now. That was what he was going to propose the next day.

But what happened when he got to the Paulson's vintage farmhouse was something completely different than Michael had anticipated. It had all begun innocently enough. Millie had settled into a chair, and Michael sat at the end of a large couch in the living room. Then he told her what was on his mind. She listened thoughtfully without saying a word.

Finally, Millie got up and walked toward him. She sat down next to him and he could smell her perfume and feel the heat of her body, which was welcome on this cool late October day. She turned to him, looked into his eyes, and spoke.

"If that is what you truly want, Michael," she said softly as she put her hand on his leg, just above his knee.

"It's not, Millie. I think you know that."

Her hand slid further up his leg, making him take a deep breath.

"Millie," he said in a whisper, and took her hand off his leg. But instead of putting it down, he brought it to his face. The next thing he knew, he was kissing her hand, then kissing her lips.

Two months of pent-up desire for Millie were just too much for Michael. It had been months since he and his wife had engaged in marital relations, and between that and his strong feelings for Millie, he forgot everything he said he was going to do that day, and things went in a completely different direction. Millie loosened his tie and Michael pulled it off wildly, dropping it to the floor. They quickly undressed one another, and were lost in passion.

***

That night as Michael said his prayers, he prayed for himself, and for Millie. He didn't know quite what to do. He had never done anything like this in his life, and he was quite sure Millie had not either. He loved Millie. So, now what was he going to do? Maybe Diane had been right to suggest he go into a completely different field of work, because that was probably what was going to have to happen in the future. He would probably have to file for a divorce, and in his mind, he thought Diane might not be opposed to that idea, given the way she had been acting over the past year, and especially the past few months.

However, he knew this was not the time to make such a decision. Advent and Christmas were right around the corner. He would pray about it in the meantime, then make some kind of plan after Christmas was over. Even if things were different with Millie by then, he knew things would never be the same between him and Diane again, even if she never found out what he had done.

He no longer loved his wife. The thought made him

feel sad and full of shame. But it couldn't change his mind or heart. Unfortunately, Michael didn't think they could ever find again what they had once shared. He finished his prayer and did his devotions, then took a shower before he went to bed. He could smell Millie all over himself, and if he could smell her, then his wife most likely could as well.

***

Over the next few days, Diane noticed a change in her husband. It was subtle, but welcome. He seemed to be happier and more at peace than he had in a long time. She noticed, too, when he left his laptop open in the living room, that he had been Googling information on how to become a life coach, and about master's programs in counseling. He had once talked about getting certified as a counselor as something he'd be interested in doing in the future, perhaps in retirement, and it would help his ministry counseling skills as well.

Maybe he was finally coming around to her suggestions that they both do something different in the future. The thought made her excited and happy—until she got a call from Charles Paulson.

***

Charles had been on the road in Nebraska and Kansas for a week. He expected Millicent to greet him, but instead, he returned to a quiet, empty farmhouse. A note on the counter informed him that Millie was at church working on some special music with Evelyn Russo. Charles wasn't disappointed to be alone. He was looking forward to relaxing and reading a book he had picked up in the airport. He sat down in his favorite reading chair and started opening the book when something under the couch, which was directly across from him, caught his eye.

He tried to forget about it, but he was too "OCD" for that. He sighed and got up from the velvety chair and crouched down in front of the couch. He swept his hand under it and pulled out a man's tie. It was not his, but he recognized it.

He wondered what to do first. Would he ask Millie about it when she got home? But instead, he decided he would speak with Diane, as he was pretty sure the tie belonged to her husband. If it did, they could decide together how to handle what appeared to be some level of infidelity on the part of their spouses. If it didn't belong to the pastor, then he would confront Millie straight on about it.

He dialed Diane's number. He wouldn't tell her what he wanted to talk about on the phone, so they decided to meet the next day in private. Diane suggested they meet at their family cabin, which was only a few miles from the farmhouse. Together, maybe they could get to the bottom of this, and figure out their next moves if it was indeed what he thought *it* was.

***

Diane took one look at the tie and a curious look crossed her face. "How did you get that?"

"I found it," Charles said. "Under the couch in my living room."

It took a moment for this to sink in. Diane had always thought that if something like this happened to her, she would be devastated. That was back when her and Michael's relationship was solid. Now, it only made her angry and embarrassed.

Charles seemed to be in the same camp as well, as anger welled up in his face and he slammed a fist on the table. He apologized profusely, and Diane reassured him he had every right to feel angry, putting her hand on his in empathy.

They sat at the table and talked for a long time, both admitting their marriages were failing. Diane could hardly believe Millie would do such a thing to someone as wonderful as Charles. He had always been such a gentleman and a hard worker. She had almost asked him to a Sadie Hawkins dance once in high school, as she thought he was the smartest person in the school. She also loved his fair hair and complexion, along with his air of sophistication. She had hoped he would ask her out, but thought he was out of her league.

Charles equally couldn't believe Michael would do this to Diane. She was kind, beautiful, did so much for the church, and most of all was the mother of Michael's child. Charles couldn't understand such a betrayal of both wife and daughter.

Both Charles and Diane needed to get home and stood up from the table.

"What do we do now?" Diane asked.

"I'm not sure yet. Let me think about it—and let's see what happens. Maybe this was a one-time fling, but unfortunately, I perceive otherwise. Millicent appeared absolutely giddy when I arrived home," Charles said.

Diane thought about Michael's recent behavior and his new and improved attitude. Now she had an explanation—it just wasn't the one she had been anticipating or wanting.

Diane sighed. "Thank you for contacting me, Charles." She suddenly felt very vulnerable, and a look of hurt flashed across her face.

"You don't deserve this type of treatment, Diane," Charles said, and then proceeded to hug her gently.

It felt good to be in the arms—if only for a moment—of someone who actually cared about her and thought she was special.

"Neither do you, Charles."

They looked at each other a long moment, then let go and were on their ways back to their respective houses and spouses.

***

Charles and Diane met at the same time at the cabin every week that month after their initial meeting, reporting on their spouses and just talking. They both thought whatever happened between their spouses may have been a one-time occurrence. They even decided it could have been a more innocent situation, where Michael was uncomfortable, took off his tie, and it fell to the floor and he forgot about it.

Diane and Charles watched their spouses every Wednesday night and Sunday morning for any clues that anything was going on. Diane smelled her husband's dirty shirts in the laundry hamper every night after he fell asleep, but hadn't smelled the perfume again.

She and Charles decided they no longer needed to

meet at the cabin, even though Diane had to admit she would miss their visits. Charles was so kind and caring, and so easy to talk to. He really listened to her, and gave her much-needed encouragement.

It was getting close to Christmas and there were so many things to do, which made it easier to forget about Millie and Michael. Charles had one more out-of-town trip before Christmas, and another one right after, just before the annual choir party at his and Millie's house. Diane had many church obligations, the biggest being a tea she hosted the first Saturday of Advent for the women of the congregation. It was well-attended and Diane usually enjoyed it, but she was just too burned out on too many fronts to get excited about it this year. At least it kept her mind off recent events—that is, until she received another call from Charles, one that would rock her world like none other.

***

Charles gathered up the trash receptacles from around the house, emptying them into the large container he would dump into the burn barrel out back. It was a cold afternoon, and almost dark out. He hated the loss of sunlight at this time of year.

He turned the container into the barrel, pushing it down with the top of the can. He didn't see it at first, but all of a sudden he stopped dead in his tracks. He dug through some disgusting paper tissues and dental floss, and there it was. Wrapped in some toilet tissue, just one tiny end of plastic stuck out. At first he thought it was a feminine product, but it was flatter than that.

He pulled the tissue away. It was a pregnancy test—he knew that from the many times he and Millicent had used them, hoping to learn they would be parents. This time the little symbol on it indicated it was positive. Millicent—was pregnant.

***

Millie was more tired than she had ever been in her life, yet she had never felt so happy and energized. It was a strange combination of feelings. She felt a bit queasy in the mornings, and her breasts were sore and sensitive, but otherwise, she felt amazing. Her dream of becoming a mother was finally coming true. Now, how to break the news was another thing. She also wanted to make sure the pregnancy was viable. With all the trouble she had experienced getting pregnant, she was wary of the store-bought test's results. She also worried she might miscarry. One doctor they had seen said she may have had an early-pregnancy miscarriage at some point, yet another said it was unlikely.

She decided to think and pray, then make a plan to announce her news by the end of the calendar year, which was only weeks away. There were many worship services to prepare for, all with special music, and then, of course, her favorite event of the year, the choir party between Christmas and New Year's. She would decorate her house this year like none other, as she was feeling quite celebratory. She even ordered some new decorations for each room on the main floor of the house. This would be the best Christmas and best choir party ever.

***

Charles was happy to be gone for business before Christmas. He couldn't stand to watch Millicent decorating the house with that huge grin on her face. She even purchased new decorations. He wondered how much that cost him.

He put up the main tree—a live Frasier fir—from the grove he and his parents had planted—and which he had kept planting since his move back—on the back acres of the farm. It graced the living room, and he carefully strung it with lights, as his father had before him. He put heirloom ornaments on it and would put popcorn and cranberries on it just before Christmas Eve.

The rest of the artificial trees that Millicent insisted on having in every room were up to her to decorate. He always hoped that might dissuade her, but it never did. She took such pleasure in making each one unique, and she did have an eye for decorating, which was the only thing that made them tolerable to Charles. Otherwise, he saw them as unnecessary clutter.

She hadn't said a word about the pregnancy test, and he thought perhaps she was waiting until Christmas to share the news. He wondered what else she would have to say at that time. In the meantime, he had made a decision. He would not be there for her choir party, no matter what. He would make up some type of excuse. It had happened before that his meetings or other business were extended, so she wouldn't be that surprised if he was delayed. He was in no mood to help her out.

***

The night of the party and Millie's death

Millie smoothed her bright red dress down her front. Her hand stopped just below her navel. She wondered how long it would be before she "showed." She had imagined this scenario for years, but had given up hope of it ever becoming a reality. Millie had felt queasy the past few mornings, and the smell and taste of coffee—one of her favorite things—was disgusting to her. But that was okay. She was going to be a mother—finally. She was already in love with her baby—and she was in love with his or her father. Millie beamed at her reflection in the full-length mirror in the bedroom, then headed downstairs to uncover her goodies and begin to greet guests.

She was excited about the party, but that wasn't all. She had made up her mind. She would share her news tomorrow. It would have been sooner, but Charles had called earlier to say his flight was canceled due to the snowstorm which was hitting Omaha, and would arrive in their area around the time her gathering was over. She only hoped the storm wouldn't come in earlier than expected and ruin the night.

By seven, everyone was in attendance. As usual, Pastor Michael said a prayer thanking the Lord for the food and for the gifts the members of the choir shared throughout the year, and for Millie leading them. She could feel herself blush as he prayed. Then they sang the congregation's favorite, "Be present at our table, Lord..." which was a tradition Millie adored.

The group filled their plates and glasses, ate and

drank...and ate and drank, then milled about the house looking at the decorations, which were particularly outstanding this year, or gathered in twos or threes to talk.

At one point in the evening, Millie found herself at the kitchen counter with just Pastor Michael. They had been very careful not to be found alone together over the past two months, ever since his visit to the farmhouse. But tonight, she just didn't care anymore.

"I have something to tell you—tomorrow," she said in a whisper.

Michael was truly hoping she wasn't going to tell him she was resigning or moving away.

"Is everything okay?" he asked quietly.

She nodded affirmatively. "Would five o'clock in your office work?" Millie knew that Margaret would be gone by then, and she would have had a chance to see Charles first, who said he would be on the earliest flight out he could get the next morning.

Millie smiled at him sweetly, then moved away before anyone else could see the love in her eyes.

***

Millie finally cleaned up the mess in the kitchen and went upstairs. If she thought she had been tired before from the pregnancy, she now knew a new level of weariness. She finished brushing her teeth and had put a washcloth to her face. The old house was creaking and shaking because of the storm brewing outside, and it was freaking her out.

Millie looked up, saw an image in the mirror, and gasped as something red and blue wrapped tightly around her neck. She pulled at it, to no avail. She saw a familiar face in the mirror, but for some reason, it would not help her—rather, it belonged to the one who was hurting her.

She struggled, then found herself feeling like she was floating, or perhaps in a dream. It only lasted minutes. Millie saw her mom and dad's smiling faces for the first time in many years. There was a bright light, and then everything went black.

***

The day after Millie's death

Charles Paulson's hand shook as he dialed 9-1-1. He thought he might get the State Patrol, but instead he got that inept Joe Zimmerman; perhaps that was for the best. It didn't really matter anyway. What was done, was done. Millicent was dead. There was nothing anyone could do to bring her back to life.

***

Diane had answered the doorbell at the parsonage. Michael was just getting a cup of coffee, then he was going to head back to church. He thought perhaps it was one of the many parishioners who stopped by from time to time, but instead, it was Sgt. Joe Zimmerman. Joe's grandma had been a member at St. John's, but Michael had rarely seen Joe in church since her death.

He heard Joe mention Millie's name. Then the words he would never forget. Millie was dead. As the words registered, the coffee cup in his hand slipped and broke on the hardwood floor of the living room. He felt like he was breaking right with it. He thought he might pass out—or even die. In some ways, he wished he was dead.

Present Day

Joe Zimmerman reopened the file on Millicent Paulson's murder, looking for information on Charles. He found that someone had called the airlines and confirmed that his flight was canceled. They checked to see that he had rented a car one-way back to the Madison airport and picked up his car from there. What they had missed was the date. Everything was one day earlier than Charles had said. He rented the vehicle early in the morning of December 28th, not the 29th, and picked up his car in Madison early in the evening.

Joe stared straight ahead. Charles was back in the state at the time of the murder. He hadn't gone home to help Millie with the party, though. Everyone mentioned he was not there. But he could have been there afterward. He could have been home in time to stop whomever killed Millie. Or—he could have done it himself? But what about the suicide note and death of Pastor Michael?

Joe decided he was going to ask Diane one more time about what Pastor Michael had done after the party. She had mentioned she went to bed, then he went to do his prayers and devotions. It was presumed he had gone back to the Paulson's home after Diane fell asleep, and killed Millie. There was no sign of forced entry, though. But maybe she was expecting him to come back, with Charles being out of town? If they were having an affair, it was a possibility. Would he have gone back and found out she was pregnant and wanted to get rid of her because of it? There were so many questions in Joe's mind.

He was driving out in the area near the Paulson's and Diane's when all this crossed his mind. He decided he would just stop in and ask her. He wanted to see her anyway, as she was almost always on his mind.

He pulled into the gravel lane to Diane's cabin, having found out which property was hers thanks to Simon. The driveway was bumpy and needed a new load of gravel and a grader. It sure was a beautiful spot, though, and he could understand how it would have been a great "staycation" spot. As he pulled around the corner toward the house, he stopped short. There were two cars parked at the house. One was Diane's. The other he recognized, too. It belonged to Charles Paulson.

He parked his cruiser and quietly shut the door. His heart was pounding. If Charles had been the one to hurt Millie, might he also hurt Diane? Joe walked to the front window, looking into a living room with an impressive stone fireplace, but no people. He walked to another window, which turned out to look into the kitchen— again, no one. He walked around to the back of the house and slowly and carefully moved his head so he could see into the bedroom window. The blinds were open, as there was nothing but woods behind it. Joe had to stifle a gasp. He couldn't believe what he saw.

***

The day leading up to Millie's death

Charles Paulson rented the last SUV available at the

car rental agency on December 28th. He wasn't sure he would have made it back to Madison in time had he not gotten a four-wheel-drive vehicle. In fact, the road had closed in Nebraska not long after his departure.

It had been a very unpleasant drive back to Wisconsin, but he finally made it. He returned his rent-a-car and picked up his own SUV, happy to be in a familiar vehicle. At least the storm hadn't hit home yet, so he could get to his destination with little trouble. He drove into the long gravel driveway around nine o'clock that evening, unlocked the cabin door, and waited inside until he got a text.

The snow was falling fast when he left. Luckily, he had driven his driveway so many times he could have done it in his sleep. He tried the front door, sure it would have been locked. It wasn't, however, which was unusual, but welcome on this occasion. He didn't even have to get out his key, which was great, as he wanted to make as little noise as possible.

The old wooden stairs creaked as he ascended them, but the rattling of the old farmhouse helped cover them up. It was fortuitous that Millicent was still in the bathroom when he reached the top of the stairs. It made what he had come home to do just that much easier. He took the red and blue tie from his pocket and stepped into the room behind her.

He had been irate. He had been irate with Millicent. He couldn't believe she had put him in this position. She was pregnant with another man's child—the pastor's, no less. He knew it was barely possible for him to father a child, but most of all, he knew he hadn't slept with his wife in over four months. If this got out, or Millie did something crazy like leaving him (she had told him she wanted to talk to him when he returned from his trip), not only would everyone know his wife had cheated on him, but his family's name would be dragged through the mud all over town and his home church. That was completely unacceptable.

It had all been over in about five minutes, then he quietly left and drove back to the cabin only a couple miles from his house, where he spent the night and waited until early the next afternoon. Everything had worked like clockwork. He had thought it would all be a done deal.

But after Pastor Michael heard that Millie had been pregnant, there was a new problem. Diane told Charles he was inconsolable. He must have known that Charles was not the father, but rather the child was his. What if he brought this to the authorities? Something had to be done.

Charles and Diane had missed their meetings at the cabin, so after a couple of weeks, they started them up again. After discovering Millie's pregnancy, Charles had asked Diane for his own key to the cabin. He didn't really want her to know what he was planning at first, as he had wanted to keep her out of it. But he also knew he needed help to make his plan come off without a hitch, so he had asked her to text him when everyone had left the party. Diane made sure she and Michael were the last ones to leave that night, and she texted Charles as soon as she got home and Michael had gone to his study. Diane was happy to help Charles, because an unexpected thing had occurred. She and Charles had fallen in love with one another.

After Michael's devastated reaction to Millicent's pregnancy, Diane was the one to bring up what she referred to as "the next step." Now it was her turn to be hurt and angry. She was so angry with Michael. Not only had he cheated on her, but did so with an employee and a member of the church. If this were found out, he would be taken off the clergy roster, losing everything he—and *she*— had worked for over so many years. All those hours of volunteering and heading up committees! And there was absolutely no way she was going to stand for the public humiliation she would face if this were to get out. So, she and Charles put their heads together.

***

The day of Pastor Michael's death

Diane's plan was to go to quilting that morning, but before she left, she put Michael's favorite Irish whiskey, which she had just purchased, out on the kitchen counter. Then she made sure he knew it was there. She made a fresh pot of coffee and put it in a carafe, and suggested he relax and treat himself to some Irish coffee.

Michael had been moping for months now, and she was tired of seeing him pining away for the person with whom he had been unfaithful to her. She knew from past experience that he could not control himself if he started drinking this particular whiskey, and she was right again that day.

She had given Charles a key to the back door of her house in case it was locked. She had purposely left it unlocked, and doubted Michael would check it, but she wanted to make certain Charles could get in if it was.

Charles watched the whiskey bottle from the back door window, and it went down and down very quickly. When he no longer saw Michael come back for a drink, he crept into the house and saw him passed out in his chair. He texted Diane a friendly hello, which was the signal for her to come home. She did, and together they got Michael into position, with Diane pushing the stool from underneath his feet.

Diane had typed the suicide note on the computer, as she had access to Michael's office keys and knew his password—Addie2000. It had been the perfect plan, and all seemed to be working—and would have—if it hadn't been for that damn Joe Zimmerman.

***

Present day

Joe called for backup, and went around to the front of Diane's house in the woods. He waited for another officer and a trooper to arrive, both with no sirens. They parked in the driveway, keeping their vehicles out of sight. They joined Joe and gathered together at the front door. Joe knocked. He wasn't necessarily going to arrest anyone, but he was going to bring Charles Paulson in for questioning. The backup was to ensure proper cooperation, for the most part.

Diane came to the door a few minutes later. Joe had expected it to take a while for her to come to the door.

When he had looked in the back bedroom window, he had seen Diane and Charles unclothed and in bed together—having sex. He had felt like vomiting.

Joe told Diane he wanted to talk to Charles, and that he knew he was there. Charles could come out willingly, or Joe would go in and find him.

Just then, Joe heard a gun fire. He pulled out his weapon, thinking they were being shot at, but there were no more shots fired, just silence. Joe rushed to the back bedroom, where he found Charles on the floor in his underwear, a gunshot to his head. The trooper had run right behind Joe and was calling for an ambulance. Diane ran back as well. She had screamed, then shouted to Charles not to die and leave her, and that she loved him.

It had been hard for Joe to witness, frankly, but he did a good job of tuning it out and acting professionally. The ambulance arrived, and they took Charles away. He was still alive, and they thought he had a decent chance of living. Charles was not proficient with a gun. He didn't own one, but had found the pistol in the nightstand. Luckily for him, he wasn't a very good shot and it was a small-caliber weapon.

Joe turned the situation over to the other deputy, as he was too personally involved. He now realized that he had been played by Diane—that she had just been "keeping her enemies close," as they say. He thought back to all the times he had mentioned other possibilities of who may have killed Millie, only for the subject to be changed, or to be asked to dinner or some other outing with her as a distraction. It all seemed so clear now, but he hadn't seen it earlier because he was in love with her. Now he saw what he should have seen all along, and he was filled with emotions. He was hurt. He was disappointed. He was angry.

There was nothing they could really prove at that point, and Diane wasn't talking except to answer a few basic questions. She told them the gun was hers; she kept it for personal protection in the drawer next to her bed. And no, she didn't know why Charles had shot himself. The officer carefully put the weapon in a bag for evidence, and told Diane she should not leave the area, as she might be brought in for more questioning in the near future.

Joe went back to his cruiser and got out of there as quickly as he could. He felt like he couldn't breathe. He never felt as hurt or as used as he did when he left the cabin. He didn't know exactly what Charles had done, but now he was more suspicious than ever, since Charles had been willing to kill himself rather than be interviewed by the authorities.

Joe went home that evening and cracked open a beer. He wasn't about to go back to his old ways of eating and drinking, but he just couldn't do a workout right then and there. He couldn't shake the image of Diane and Charles together in bed, or her shouting to Charles that she loved him.

Joe put a ball game on the television, but he didn't really watch it. The beer made him sleepy, which was welcome. He went to bed, trying not to think about how he had been manipulated by Diane, and what more he might discover in the future. The hospital in Madison contacted him saying that Charles should survive, and would probably be available to be interviewed in a few days.

Joe had filed a report on the incident, and also reported

the new information about Charles to his superiors in person. He told them what he had learned about Charles, leading him to want to question him in the future, and making him want to warn Diane. He hadn't expected Charles to be at Diane's when he went to her home to talk to her.

Another investigator was going to take over the case, as Joe explained his relationship to Diane, who was also in a relationship with the person in question. It was for the best, he knew. It had been quite the eight months. At least he knew his instincts were still there—at least somewhat. They sure had been off about Diane, but in that case, he had been blinded by what he had believed to be love. But in Charles' case, he was glad he took one last look at his file. It would be interesting to see what the new investigator would find.

***

Ten months later, Joe Zimmerman sat at an outdoor patio table at a restaurant on Lake Monona in Madison. He held the hand of his colleague and lunch date, Jodie, whom he had been seeing for the past two months. He had been wary to venture into the area of love again, but Jodie was just too nice and too amazing to not give it a try. Over the past eight months, she had often met him for coffee to discuss cases, and he really started to know her, and like her. She was older than he had originally thought her to be, as she had worked in the Lutheran Volunteer Corps for two years before she went to college for criminal justice.

She was a unique combination of pretty, smart, kind, strong, a good cop, and came from a solid family. She recently introduced him to her parents at a cookout at their house northeast of Madison, and he had come away with a good feeling about it, as had her folks. Her parents had been a bit wary that she was dating someone ten years older than she was, but Joe felt and acted ten years younger than he was, now that he led a healthy lifestyle. He had impressed Jodie's parents, much to his happy surprise.

In a few weeks, Joe and Jodie were going away for a long weekend up north. Joe was finally using some time off and some of that money he had been saving for travel. It wasn't a very exotic outing, but it was a start, and a first for him.

Charles Paulson had been convicted on three counts of first-degree murder. He had blabbed to the new investigator right away, and threw Diane "under the bus" as well, telling of her involvement in the murders, especially of her husband's. So much for true love. Diane was convicted of one count of first-degree murder, in the case of Michael's death, and as an accessory to first-degree murder in the case of Millicent's death. She had been the one who texted Charles when everyone had left the party, and also gave him a place to wait and stay before and after he killed Millicent. Both she and Charles were now serving prison sentences.

Charles was sentenced to three life sentences, with no parole. Joe wondered how long Charles would even last in prison with his fair, pretty boy looks and his arrogant attitude, having killed a member of the clergy. Diane would be eligible for parole in ten years. She had sent St. John's a sincere letter of apology, as well as one to her daughter, and one to Joe, which had been unexpected. She had become involved in the prison Bible study, and quickly became a leader in the group.

Addie was still in college, engaged in therapy, and was trying to learn to forgive her mother. She went home to her paternal grandparents' home in northern Wisconsin when not in school or working at the Bible Camp. She once had planned to go to seminary like her dad, but she didn't feel ready to pursue that yet. So she planned to go on in school after her undergraduate degree for a Ph.D. at the University of Wisconsin to become a psychiatrist. Joe figured she was probably searching for answers, as were many in Farmerton.

Despite being relentlessly pursued by Donald Tripp, Janie Johnson couldn't accept the news that Charles didn't really love her. Instead, she wrote to him almost every day, and Joe recently heard that she even drove hours to visit him at the maximum-security prison on the other side of the state. He guessed she really loved Charles, but felt sorry for her, as Charles would never set foot outside prison walls again, and most of all because he doubted Charles Paulson could ever really love anyone other than himself.

St. John's still had Pastor Kate as their interim pastor, and she would stay with them until more healing occurred. They had been progressing well, but the latest revelations set them back again, naturally. Edward still played the organ, provided special music, and tried to rebuild a small choir. It would be quite the challenge. And Oscar still grumpily cleaned the church every week.

Jared hit a deer not long after his traffic stop and totaled his beautiful new truck. He did not replace it with another truck, but instead bought an old beater car. The rest of the money he received from the insurance company he donated to the church, never giving an explanation as to why. He started going back to church and singing with the new little choir. Edward was so desperate, he let Jared play the guitar in church, even doing a guitar and piano praise song duet together one Sunday. In general, Jared felt much better than he had in a very long time.

Simon and Gordon had good fortune smile on them both. Charles' parents were granted rights to the farm, as Charles was serving life sentences without parole, and had no wife or dependents to which to leave the property. They sold Simon the thirty acres of land he had wanted, and he was right on it to develop it. Simon also was asked to sell Diane's country home and property. Between the two, Simon made more money than ever before. He even made enough to buy one of the plots out on the farmland and build a house on it, much to his sister's delight. This good fortune was also helpful in him keeping his sobriety, along with the rehab program he had recently finished.

The elder Paulsons sold Gordon Roth the rest of the farm. They couldn't face going back to the property after what had transpired there—what their only son had done on the premises. Gleefully, Gordon and his wife lived in the old farmhouse, Gordon feeling like it was some kind of cosmic payback for the way his ancestors had been treated by the Paulson family long ago.

Evelyn Russo moved to Madison, found a new position as an organist in a huge church, and met a lovely musician who eventually became her partner. She no longer returned to St. John's cemetery to Millie's grave afterward.

Margaret Miller left Farmerton. She never got over being interviewed about the vandalization of the church

office. During the murder investigations, Diane had confessed to doing the damage at the church. She had gone
back to the office that afternoon after the church picnic, as
she still had her husband's keys to the offices. It had been
the one-year anniversary of the hug between her husband
and Millie at the previous year's picnic, which had started
everything. When she had typed Pastor Michael's supposed
suicide note, she truly meant it when she wrote that he
was responsible for Millie's death. In her mind, he was.

So even though Diane had confessed and any suspicions
about Margaret were cleared, Margaret was so hurt she
just couldn't go on living in the town she had lived in most
of her life. She felt betrayed, and decided to live in another
small town where some of her family resided.

***

Joe and Jodie paid the bill at the restaurant, then held
hands as they walked back to Joe's car. It was a gorgeous
day, with a gentle breeze, just-right temperature, and low
humidity. They would have loved to take a long walk near
the shore, but unfortunately, they had to head right back
to Farmerton, as Joe had to work a three-to-eleven shift
that evening— vacation season again. But he smiled as he
remembered that soon it would be his turn to be off.

***

As Joe drove through Farmerton and out into the
country that evening on his shift, he thought about his
lunch on the lake with Jodie. It had been a beautiful,
perfect day. He also thought about how it was fun to visit

other places, but despite all that had happened in his little town recently, it was, and would always be, home. It was a good town, full of good, yet flawed, human beings, himself included.

Joe knew that everyone had something hidden in their secret heart. Most were just little things, but every once in a while there was something bigger, like there had been this past year. He was certainly glad events like those were anomalies, and not regularities.

Joe sighed a happy and contented sigh, took out his thermos of coffee, and poured himself a cup. Sure enough, he got a call to respond to a "fender-bender" the moment he put the cup to his lips. He swore, dumped the hot coffee out the window, put on his lights and sirens, and was on his way to save another day.

The End

About Atmosphere Press

Atmosphere Press is an independent, full-service publisher for excellent books in all genres and for all audiences. Learn more about what we do at atmospherepress.com.

We encourage you to check out some of Atmosphere's latest releases, which are available at Amazon.com and via order from your local bookstore:

The Embers of Tradition, a novel by Chukwudum Okeke

Saints and Martyrs: A Novel, by Aaron Roe

When I Am Ashes, a novel by Amber Rose

Melancholy Vision: A Revolution Series Novel, by L.C. Hamilton

The Recoleta Stories, by Bryon Esmond Butler

Voodoo Hideaway, a novel by Vance Cariaga

Hart Street and Main, a novel by Tabitha Sprunger

The Weed Lady, a novel by Shea R. Embry

A Book of Life, a novel by David Ellis

It Was Called a Home, a novel by Brian Nisun

Grace, a novel by Nancy Allen

Shifted, a novel by KristaLyn A. Vetovich

About the Author

Kathy J. Jacobson is a graduate of the University of Wisconsin and Wartburg Theological Seminary. Kathy worked with troubled youth in the juvenile justice system for ten years. Later, she worked in campus and rural ministry, as well as volunteering as a hospice chaplain. She currently lives in Monona, Wisconsin with her husband. They have three grown children and three grandchildren. She has traveled to six continents and all fifty states. In addition to traveling, she loves hiking, the Wisconsin Badgers, and, most of all—writing! Kathy recently authored the five-book *Noted!* fiction series. *In The Secret Heart* is her debut mystery novel.

Author's note—

In the Secret Heart is a work of fiction. All of the events, characters, and places in this novel are either used fictitiously or are products of my imagination.

As always, I am thankful for the stellar support and encouragement of my family, friends, and fans in my writing ventures.